THE
ADVENTURES
OF
ROBIN HOOD

by

MAJOR CHARLES GILSON

THE CHILDREN'S PRESS
LONDON AND GLASGOW

This Impression 1976

ISBN 0 00 166019 5

PRINTED AND MADE IN GREAT BRITAIN

CONTENTS

CHAPTER ONE

SAXON THANE AND NORMAN BARON

WHEN Duke William of Normandy conquered and slew King Harold at Senlac, the England that we know to-day had even then been for centuries in the making. For he who calls himself British may belong to a so-called mongrel race; but it is to be remembered that the blood that flows in his veins is that of many conquering adventurers who, one after the other, thought these islands well worthy of winning.

First came the man of the New Stone Age, of whom we know but little, save that he had both intelligence and prowess enough to oust from his caves the ape-like aboriginal who was here before him. And after him, the Celt, one nation after another: Gael, Scot, Pict and Briton—during which time there had sprung up upon the Mediterranean shores various ancient civilisations which advanced westward through the ages, from the Persian Gulf even to the shores of Spain. As Babylon and Assyria had fallen, so, too, in turn fell Macedon, Greece and Carthage—and they fell like ancient withered trees before the might and majesty of Rome.

We all know that the Romans were here, this side of the Tweed, for four hundred years, but few realise what that means: in the first place, they were Romans from Rome, not paid legionaries from Gaul; they intermarried with the Briton, and during that long and prosperous period the country became even more civilised than it was before; Christianity replaced the savage Druidical rites, and the land was both strong and safe.

Then Rome fell, like Babylon and Carthage before, but Roman blood remained in the veins of the Britons who were harried from Thanet to the Thames and thence north to Trent by the barbarians who had come down from the Baltic Sea, like eagles swooping on their quarry. Saxons, Jutes and Angles these new invaders called themselves, fair-haired giants, blue of eye, who knew naught of mercy and who worshipped Pagan gods. Right and left, east and west, they slew; but in a thickly populated country there were many Britons who survived who had not sought refuge in the Welsh mountains or the red hills of Cornwall.

Another four hundred years passed—and one has to realise that this is the same period that has elapsed from early Tudor times until the present day—and the Saxons had forsaken Thor and Wodin for the Christ and the sword and buckler for the ploughshare. So for a thousand years or more it had been war and peace, with the blood of these conquerors forming a nation that was still to be, a language the richest in the world, and a breed of men who were to carry their flag, their trade, their culture, and above all their sense of liberty and justice, to the uttermost parts of the earth.

Passing over yet another invasion by the Danes, it was not until the end of these thousand years that there came to these shores the greatest victor of all—William, Duke of Normandy, of whom we have written in the very first line of the story we have now to tell. It is a story of England, not the England that we know to-day, but a land in which the Norman was the overlord and master and the Saxon the vanquished, who yet thought of himself as "English" and of the country as his own.

It took a great deal longer than two hundred years for these two nations to blend, to found a common language, to have common interests and ideals, and to fight for the same common cause against a common foe, from Agincourt to Ypres. Those first two centuries of our history were troublous times of strife, poverty and oppression. The Saxons had their own customs, dress and form of government. Under the Saxon kings there had been earls, thanes, freemen and serfs, and all these—even the last—had their own pride and love of country. Duke William, strong in mind as he was strong of arm, had established law and order with an iron hand. By the feudal system the Norman barons, to whom he had parcelled out the land, were as much his vassals as the Saxon thane had been to any Saxon king; and among these Saxon nobles was one, Alfred of Sherwood, whose forebear of the same name had driven back the Danes when they had come south to Derby.

For that stout service the thanes of Sherwood had been granted all the manors that lay on either bank of the Trent; and it was said, before William came, that the forest east of Nottingham and the pleasant vale of Newstead was the very heart of Saxon-Danish England.

That Alfred, Earl of Sherwood, had never fought at Hastings, since he had been sorely wounded in the fight at Stamford Bridge against the Northmen and Harold's traitor brother. Afterwards, if he swore fealty to the Conqueror, he did so only to spare the lives of good men and true, and because he was wise enough to recognise that, with the death of Harold, the Saxon cause was lost. For he had seen the Norman armies march north into Mercia; and though there were many among his foresters and bondmen who would willingly have fought and died, there was more wisdom under his grey hairs than in the hotheads who thought Merry Sherwood greater than all Normandy and Anjou.

"Could I but stay the Trent in flood with the palm of a hand," he told them, "then would we avenge King Harold and reclaim our England for our own. But what can it avail for the wounded stag to turn against the hounds? Therefore, whatever befall this fair land that our forebears won by right of conquest, henceforward let the stag be our standard and our emblem. Though we be vanquished, yet can we hold high our heads. And who hath a prouder head than a stag of Sherwood Forest?"

So there came a Norman overlord to hold dominion and to owe fealty to Duke William from the wild moors by Sheffield to Charnwood, from Dove Dale to the Trent; and the name of this man was Roger Braisse-Neuve, Baron of Normanton by Derby where the Danes had been. Thus the Norman baron was the prince of the Saxon thane, whom he called a "franklin"; a sheriff was appointed for each shire, and all the manors in the land paid their taxes to the Crown.

Now that was in the reign of William, when a strong mailed hand held all England in thrall from the Channel coast to the wall the Romans had built; but, after the civil strife in Stephen's time, when the whole country was troubled and disordered, much of the good work done by Henry the Second, who strove to unite the Saxon and the Norman, went by the board, when

Richard, the Lion-heart, thought more of slaying Saracen Turks than making friends with honest English yeomen.

"When the cat's away, the mice will play"—and that was so in Richard's time, for of the five years he reigned he spent but one in England; and during the absence of this warlike prince, who was more a knight-errant than a monarch, there was not a baron in the land who did not think himself as good as any king. Another Alfred then held the former earldom of Sherwood; and this thane, no longer in his first youth, with his earls, freemen and serfs from Barnesdale to Sherwood Forest, was the vassal of one, Robert Braisse-Neuve, whom even his own Norman men-at-arms called Robert the Wolf. For he looked like a wolf, and he had the heart and fangs of a wolf; and never had there been an overlord of Sherwood more hated and feared.

It was he who built a strong castle at Normanton by Derby of which not a stone remains to this day; and it was as Sir Robert Braisse-Neuve, Baron Normanton and Hautbray, that he would raise the standard of Prince John, the King's weak, passionate and evil younger brother, who had promised him that, when he came to the throne, Robert le Loup would hold sway over both Norman soldiery and Saxon "slaves"— as he would have them—from the West Riding to Northampton.

Not far from Newstead, in the heart of Sherwood Forest, where the famous abbey stands even to this day, Alfred of Sherwood, the Saxon thane, lived with all his English household in a tower surrounded by a palisade—the very stronghold in which his ancestor had defied the savage Danes. And there he kept open house to all of Saxon blood. Even the very dogs that gnawed the bones upon the lime-trod floor of his banquet-hall seemed Saxon to him—hounds fit to hunt the Norman Wolf. He had a Saxon friar, though that fat and jovial man of God thought more of a haunch of venison than his rosary; and there was a minstrel, too, to sing to him—a Saxon noble-man by birth, whom they called Allen-a-Dale, for he hailed from Barnesdale.

It was a merry household, and they lived as in Saxon times, speaking their native tongue, into which there had already been introduced many foreign Norman words. Friar Tuck cracked

rude Saxon jokes, whilst he swilled horn cups of good red
French wine, patted his great paunch, and grew purple in
the face; and there was a giant among the jolly company,
whom they had named Little John; over six feet seven he
stood, as we reckon it nowadays, and it was his office to stand
warder at the outer gate, armed with a quarter-staff like a
young oak tree with which, it was said, he could crack the skull
of an ox.

There were many others of the thane's household, above
sixty souls in all, who had their home in Newstead Tower;
whilst all who lived in the surrounding forest—smith, swine-
herd, charcoal-burner, tanner and miller—were free to come
and go as they willed. For the thane gave equal welcome to
them all; and there was only one man in that part of England
who was better loved. And that was the old man's son, Robin
of Sherwood; for, if the father was admired by all as a man
whose word was his bond, it has ever been the way with
Englishmen to pay homage to one who excels all others in every
kind of manly sport and prowess.

Straight of back, strong in limb and swift of foot, Robin
was then in the pride of early manhood. Fair and bearded,
as a Saxon should be, he could use the long-bow with a skill
that made men marvel. In the great hall of Newstead Tower
he had once by rushlight shot an arrow through an apple in
the hands of Friar Tuck, at the very moment when that worthy
was about to place the fruit between his lips—which feat had
caused roars of merriment from all, save the astonished victim
of the joke, who sat there at the board shaking with fright and
gaping like a stuffed hog.

Yet no man ever was less vain than Robin. Though praising
others freely, he spoke seldom of himself. Though he, too,
could sing, and that right pleasantly, he was ready to swear
that no minstrel 'twixt the Cheviots and Chilterns had a
sweeter voice than Allen; no man alive could eat more, drink
more or laugh more heartily than Friar Tuck; and not even
Goliath himself had the strength or stature of his good friend,
Little John, who loved Robin as a great dog loves his master.

Nor, since the days of Athelstane, had there ever been a
better son at Newstead nor a worthier heir to the good estates

of Sherwood; whilst his sister, the fair Maid Marian, might have been that very Rosalind of whom Will Shakespeare was to write. For Marian, though Allen-a-Dale might love her dearly, was no damsel to sit idle in a bower, weaving tapestry and dreaming vain romantic dreams of chivalry; but, clad in buckskins, she would take to the greenwood with her brother and his merry men when, in defiance of the game laws, they went hunting over the hills of Barnesdale. More boy than girl she was, though fairer in face and complexion than the Norman maiden, the lady Beatrice Braisse-Neuve, daughter of Robert le Loup, who languished in the moated castle her sire had built upon the hill at Normanton.

As for that proud and crafty baron, when the news came to England that King Richard was a prisoner in Germany, seeing his chance to become overlord of all middle England, he decided to play a double game. If Richard was feared by his Norman subjects, baron, knight and man-at-arms, it was because he was more paladin than prince, and because no knight could stand before him either on the battlefield or in the lists. But Prince John was of another kidney: weak as water, he was ever ready to make promises he had no intention of fulfilling, and once he was crowned king, the barons knew that they would have him at their mercy. Thus was a great conspiracy hatched during Richard's absence in which many of the more powerful barons and the Knights Templar joined— and among them, it goes without saying, was Robert the Wolf, Baron Normanton and Hautbray.

Therefore he sent his heralds to Norman lord and Saxon thane alike throughout the two counties of Nottingham and Derby, ordering them to muster all their men-at-arms, archers, freemen, foresters and serfs, at Long Eaton that he might march south to Leicester, where he would swear for the nonce allegiance to Prince John—all for his own sly profit and advantage, since he knew that, once John was king, there would be no more powerful baron in the land than he.

But, to gain these ends, he was wise enough to know that he must have the support of Saxon franklin as well as Norman knight; and of the former there was none greater in all England than Alfred of Sherwood, who held the old Saxon earldom between the Derwent and the Trent. He had little doubt that the Thane of Sherwood would fall into line with the other conspirators—but there he counted a chicken that was never hatched, for he had yet to learn that there were hearts in Sherwood Forest as stout and strong as the oaks—no Norman poplar saplings to bend here and there in a wind which shifted and changed at a nod from Robert Braisse-Neuve. Therefore, when his herald came back from Newstead Manor with a message as unwelcome as unexpected, Robert le Loup swore an oath that he would teach this rude Saxon franklin a lesson that he would remember for many a day.

For the Thane of Sherwood had proved himself a good man and loyal, who would take no hand in any treachery against his overlord, the lion-hearted King, even though that king had hitherto thought little of the land he was supposed to rule. Being the last man in the world to be browbeaten by a Norman baron, Alfred of Sherwood had sent a message back to the lord of Normanton that he had sworn allegiance to a Lion and not a Wolf, and that those who served him were of the same way of thinking.

When Robert le Loup received that challenge, it was said that he unsheathed his sword with a snarl that made even his own household blanch. The churlish thane would die, he swore, by his own hand, or he would rot and be eaten alive by rats in one of the dungeons that at Normanton lay below the water-level in the moat. And thus we come, at last, to the drama of Newstead Tower that made of Robin of Sherwood an outlaw in the woods and his name famous in legend in every country in the world. Robin du Bois the hated Normans called him; but his Saxon merry men knew and loved him well by the name he took. And that was Robin Hood.

And it is his story we have now to tell. He and they who followed him stood for Merry Sherwood and the England that was passing. They may have had no flamboyant laws of chivalry and Norman honour; to them a wind on the horn in the greenwood was better than a flourish of trumpets in the lists. They hid their prowess—to quote the Scriptures, like a bright light under a bushel—in the shade of the oaks in Sherwood Forest. They favoured no plumes, save the grey goose-quill, and their cloth-yard arrows were more deadly than the lances of prancing Norman knights. They wore no mail, but good Lincoln green and the buckskin of the greenwood; and the only battle-cry they knew was no boast of their own chivalry and daring, but a brave and clear assurance of all they stood and fought for: "Saint George for Merry England."

CHAPTER TWO

NEWSTEAD TOWER

IT MUST not be imagined that the great Tower at Newstead Manor, where dwelt Alfred of Sherwood, had any of the Gothic grace, commodious arrangements or tactical strength of the Norman castle, the ruins of many of which can be seen throughout England to-day. The main fortification consisted of a central round "keep" that was exceedingly difficult of access, to which were attached several separate buildings, including the great banqueting-hall, all of which were provided in some rough measure with methods of defence such as loop-holes and embrasures for archers. There was neither moat, portcullis nor drawbridge; but the outer enclosure that corresponded to the Norman tilt-yard was surrounded by a wooden palisade of sharpened stakes and a shallow ditch that contained such obstacles as tangled brushwood. It was a Saxon edifice that had been strengthened to resist the Danes and which served at once as a manor and a castle; and there the thanes, or former earls, of Sherwood had dwelt for generations.

On the day on which this story opens there was a great feast at Newstead, on the occasion of the natal day of Maid Marian, the daughter of the manor; and as usual on all such occasions the thane kept open house. Alfred himself, grey of beard, was seated at the central oaken table, with Marian on his right and Robin on his left; and the board literally groaned beneath the weight of the good Saxon fare, whilst both wine and ale flowed freely. Friar Tuck, ever quicker to attend a banquet than a mass, had come in from the nearby hermitage, and at the head table was doing more than full justice to all the goodly provender that came within his reach. Sir Allen-a-Dale, the minstrel, was also seated in a place of honour, where he had every right to be, not only as one of noble birth, but as the betrothed of the thane's only daughter. His family having lost all their estates and money at the time of the Norman conquest, Allen had taken to minstrelsy, since he loved the strings of his harp far better than his useless purse-strings, and, as one who was Saxon born, he preferred to serve a Saxon thane than any Norman baron—though, if the truth be told, the fair Maid Marian was not the least reason why he lived at Newstead. At his side, at the high table, was one, Will Scarlock—whose name some will write as Scarlet—a kinsman of the family.

Among those at the lower table were many whom we shall meet again: Much the miller; Arthur-a-Bland, a tanner by trade; Will Stutely; Martin, the potter from Upfield, and many others who in due time were to become Robin's "Merry Men." All were there, save Little John, who kept watch and ward at the outer gate; for in those days it was not safe to leave the gate unguarded, since there were many outlaws in the forest, and fat sheep and swine grazing within the enclosure that were as good provender to ill-fed men as the Royal venison in the greenwood. Nor were the King's foresters themselves above converting a Saxon sheep into Norman mutton, though they were in Sherwood and Barnesdale to preserve the game. Little John, who as a trencherman was second only to the friar, had been promised his share of the goodly fare so soon as others could relieve him at the gate; but, for the nonce, he stood there ready with his quarter-staff, keeping a sharp lookout upon the cart-track that led to Newstead through the greenwood.

And in the meantime there approached upon the road from Nottingham a column of Norman men-at-arms, mounted and afoot, led by Robert the Wolf in person. They must have numbered six hundred in all, armed in chain mail, and in the rear came a party of torch-bearers; for Sir Robert Braisse-Neuve, knowing the strength of Newstead, meant to raze it to the ground by fire, if by chance an assault by arms should fail.

The bulk of the army—for such indeed it was—had marched

the day before from Derby, and had rested that night in Nottingham. There the baron had taken good care to call upon the Sheriff, Master Hamnett, who had the town-trained bands at his beck and call. The Sheriff, a weak man who put his own personal comfort before loyalty to the King whom England might never see again, readily espoused the cause of Prince John. For it seemed to him, as well as to many others, that it was a case of spinning a coin that must always fall the right way up, since many of the most powerful barons, the Knights Templars and all of Norman blood who had anything to gain at the crowning of Prince John were all for insurrection. If Richard, the Lion, was not shut up in a German castle, he was risking his life in the thick of a fight against Saracen Turks; and though he was known to be a warrior second to none, he who wields a battle-axe in preference to a sceptre, is even less safely seated in the saddle than on the throne. For that reason Ronald Hamnett and his trained men took the road north to Newstead from Nottingham, to oust a Saxon franklin from his manor who had dared send a challenge to the lord of Normanton and Hautbray.

The first part of their march that day led them over Bulwell Heath, and it was not until a late hour in the afternoon that they penetrated the southern part of Sherwood Forest where lay Newstead Tower. At that hour the feasting in the great hall was at its height; and there was more than one among the jolly company who had his stomach well-filled with food and his head swimming with wine. Moreover, from the twilight of the woods, this imposing armed force came suddenly upon Little John, standing guard at the gate in the palisade.

With his long legs wide-spread he challenged them, demanding the right to know who they were, whence they came and wherefore—and such defiance, as was natural enough in the circumstances, was greeted by roars of laughter. For Robert le Loup had the next thing to an army at his back, not only pikemen and those who were armed with cross-bows, but also knights a-horseback in full mail.

It was the Wolf himself who shouted his command. He was mailed from head to foot, though his visor was open and over his armour he wore the long white Norman cloak, as if he meant to take no active part in the fighting, if fighting there should be.

"Stand back, villain!" he exclaimed. "Know thou not that I am the overlord of all these domains and such as thou, including thy churlish master? Stand back, or thou art a dead man as sure as Saxon swine be the same thing as Norman pork."

One could see his long sniffing wolf-like nose and his glistening red little eyes, when he drew rein about twenty paces from the gate, having drawn aside to let his men press forward, to put a quick end to the Saxon churl of whom they thought no more than the quarter-staff he now swung skilfully and threateningly around his tousled head.

In the forefront was a mounted plumed knight in full armour who went by the name of Sir Stephen de Froy. A distant cousin of Robert Braisse-Neuve's, he held that a good enough reason why he should have joined the insurrection; but he had a more powerful motive than that to assist at the storming of Newstead Tower, and he had made no secret of the matter to the Wolf, who cared not why men served him so long as he could use them to his purpose. For de Froy had long since cast eyes on the fair maid Marian, Robin's sister and the thane's daughter; and the very circumstance that she was already affianced to Allen-a-Dale merely meant to Sir Stephen that he must take by force to the altar one who had proved as deaf to his overtures and pleas as she was unmindful of his stiff Norman pride.

"Stand aside, knave!" he shouted. "Make way for thy betters!"

But Little John gave never an inch of ground. As he was tall in stature and broad of chest, so had he a voice to match that was like the roar of a bull. Firmly planted on his feet and still swinging his quarter-staff, as if he loved the very feel of it, he now raised his voice.

"To arms!" he bellowed. "To arms! Here be the Wolf and the Norman wolfpack yelping at the gate!"

Fortunately, there was one who heard him, as shall later be described; and though Sir Stephen knew but a few words in Saxon, the warder's manner were enough to warn him that he had been defied. Close behind him was one of his esquires who carried his lance, and a certain Knight Templar, mounted, mailed and armed with a battle-axe. This man, by name Sir Geoffrey Malpert, was notorious even amongst his own Order of the Temple for his exceeding vanity. He thought himself not only the handsomest, bravest and most chivalrous of all the knights in Christendom, but the equal in strength and prowess of Richard the Lion-heart himself. Hence he carried a battle-axe that none, save the King, could have wielded; and it was to that fact alone that Little John owed his life that day.

Sir Stephen, having backed his horse, meant to clear the gateway with a charge, thinking it would prove no greater matter to cut down the gigantic warder with a drawn sword than to slice off a thistle-head with a cane.

"Look to it, varlet!" he cried. "Thou hast three seconds in which to say thy prayers before thou art dead as beef, for this be the first time I ever humbled myself by drawing sword against an ox."

With these words he charged. The sword rose and fell, like the stroke of a falcon; but Little John, despite his height and weight, sprang aside, as quick on his feet as a ferret. One end of the quarter-staff parried the sword-stroke at an angle, so that it glanced harmlessly aside, and a fraction of a second afterward, the other end of the staff caught the knight a swift and swinging blow on the side of his helmet.

There lay that valorous and skilful knight, Sir Stephen de Froy, prone and apparently senseless on the ground, upon which he had pitched head-foremost with all the weight of his armour. Nor for a second or so did he make any attempt to move, whilst his charger galloped panic-stricken through the gate.

The voice of Robert Braisse-Neuve came like the snarl of a wolf.

"He who shall be the first to slay that insolent rebel Saxon serf shall have a hundred silver crowns from my own privy purse! Am I to sit here a-horseback begging an entry at a vassal's gate? Kill the dog, and have done with it!"

Several pikemen rushed forward, each eager to claim the reward; but, being afoot, they were forestalled by Sir Geoffrey, the Templar, who was mounted and who now spurred his horse at the gate.

For Little John it were one thing to parry a sword-stroke and another to stave off a blow from a battle-axe. It must be remembered, however, that the weapon was borne more for vanity than usage, and because the knight had not strength in his arm to wield it with full effect, the blow came neither straight nor clean, and no sooner did the sharp blade meet the resistance of the quarter-staff than the haft twisted in his hand.

The staff broke in twain under the weight of the blow; but it was the flat side of the axe, instead of the blade, that caught the warder on the side of the head, and the gallant fellow dropped like a felled ox, senseless and bleeding to the ground.

"*Beau-seant!*" cried Sir Geoffrey. "For the Temple! My lord of Normanton, the way is open, though I want neither English crowns nor Venetian zecchins for my service."

As one man, Robert the Wolf, his knights and men-at-arms, rushed for the gate, jostling one another to be the first to enter, more than one of them trampling on what they took to be the corpse of Little John. Within the enclosure, where the thane's sheep were grazing, they opened out to attack the ramparts, the main body under Braisse-Neuve himself advancing upon the keep.

It was then that they received a somewhat unwelcome intimation that the walls were already manned. Four or five pikemen fell face forward, struck down by English arrows; whilst from the summit of the tower, Robin of Sherwood, with Stutely at his right hand and Will Scarlock at his left, shouted defiance, demanding by what right the baron of Normanton dared to attack the faithful subjects of King Richard to whom he himself owed a like allegiance.

"A fig for that!" cried Braisse-Neuve, seated astride his horse. "I am not here to parley with a herd of Saxon swine. As the lawful overlord of thy franklin father, I have sent him an order to muster his men under my banner, and he hath given me such an answer as I would swallow from no living man, least of all a bearded Saxon churl."

"Churl!" cried Robin. "Remember two things, or thou wilt find thyself in a fit state to remember naught. Firstly, my forebears were earls in England before ever thine were barons; and secondly, all within this castle are the faithful liegemen of King Richard, and if thou be not such, as thou art sworn, then we be no vassals of thine."

"A truce to such impudence!" Braisse-Neuve cried—and the man was stuttering with rage. "I am here for one thing and for one thing only: render up thy father or we take the place by storm, in which case the blood that may be shed shall lie upon the conscience of a rebel Saxon thane who hath dared snap his fingers at his Norman overlord!"

"Liar!" Robin shouted. "'Tis thou who art the rebel, and we are loyal men and true to a Norman sovereign, since the days be gone when an English king may be seated on the throne of England."

The Wolf turned in the saddle and waved his sword.

"For John of Anjou!" he cried. "Strike down these Saxon swine! I leave not Sherwood till I have razed this patchwork castle to the ground. Spare none, save those who admit themselves the bondmen they were all born to be. Forward, the banner of Normanton and Hautbray!"

As Braisse-Neuve's men-at-arms rushed forward like a wave, Robin bent the bow he held, took scarce aim enough for a hawk to strike its quarry, and the arrow buried its head between the joints of the baron's chain mail immediately above the heart; and had it not been for the fact that the Wolf wore a breastplate of Toledo steel under his Norman harness, the lord of Normanton and Hautbray would have dropped dead upon the spot.

CHAPTER THREE

"TO THE GREENWOOD!"

THOUGH the wolf hunts with the pack and the fox works on his own, it is the former animal that is by far the more cunning animal of the two; and Robert Braisse-Neuve, who was surnamed the Wolf, had ever lived up to his name. He had sworn to be revenged on Alfred, the Saxon; and as he had sworn that oath in public in the great hall at Normanton, he could neither rest a-bed nor have any peace of mind by day till the thane was dead and Newstead lay in ruins. Yet he was never a man who acted rashly. Though brave enough in war, he had ever been more skilful in conspiracies and plots than with his lance at tourneys. As he had now conspired against King Richard, knowing that he would be one of the greatest lords in England once John was on the throne, so he had planned with circumspection his attack on Newstead Tower.

In the first place, he was aware that his kinsman, Sir Stephen de Froy, had fallen head over heels in love with Maid Marian, the betrothed of Allen-a-Dale. A proud, passionate and wilful man, Sir Stephen was one who had been long accustomed to have his own way in all things, and moreover he was an ally whose assistance could never be despised. He had set his heart—if heart he had—upon marrying the Saxon beauty.

Though the Wolf had little of human nature in himself, he understood the thing, and he was well aware, not only of de Froy's fame in the lists and in the Holy wars with Richard, but also that there is no stronger lance nor sharper sword than that of a disgruntled and rejected lover. That he disapproved of such a match meant little or naught to him, for he had no wish to see Norman knights wedded to Saxon maidens; it was enough if he could use Sir Stephen for his purpose—and he could not be expected to foresee that the valiant knight would receive such a buffet from a quarter-staff as he would remember for many a day. But then, up to that time, Robert Braisse-Neuve was a stranger to Little John, the Newstead warder; and when he planned his assault upon the Saxon castle, that was about the only mistake he made in his crafty calculations.

Otherwise, the affair might have been a complete and sudden success, in the nature of a *coup de grâce*. For he had learnt that on that day were to be celebrated at Newstead the coming-of-age festivities of Maid Marian, and he also knew something of the nature of a Saxon feast. He knew that these short-coated, bearded churls—for so he termed them—crammed themselves with food and swilled both wine and ale till they

were too stuffed to move and their brains were swimming.
Therefore he had timed his attack, as he had thought, at the
right moment.

But it often happens that a weak point proves to be the
strongest. Stuffed to his many chins with roasted venison,
beef and swan, and having lowered manfully tankard after
tankard of the strongest wine upon the board, if there was one
man among the company who ought to have been under the
table, that man was Friar Tuck. Howbeit, the friar had a
head as strong as his arm, and the more he ate and drank, the
better man he was with either quarter-staff or cudgel. All the
same, on account of the wine that he had swallowed, which
he had mixed in honour of Maid Marian with more relish than
discretion, toward the end of the feast he had felt disposed to
cool his heated shaven pate. He had therefore betaken himself
to the battlements above the banqueting-hall, to inhale a few
draughts of good fresh air, and it was thence that he had seen
the press of Norman men-at-arms at the gateway, and he had
heard Little John's cry for help, when the gallant warder had
given the alarm.

"To arms! Here be the Wolf and the wolf-pack, yelping at
the gate!"

That was enough for the friar. His head was clear, his shaven
pate was cool; and if his belly was yet as a pipe of wine, he was
as good a man for a rough-and-tumble as was ever like to be—
and that was saying much. In less than a minute he was back
in the hall; and thus it came about that both the keep and the
ramparts were manned before ever the Wolf and his men-at-
arms had broken through the gate.

One neither can nor need describe in any detail the fight
that now raged for near upon an hour around the walls of
Newstead Manor. Sir Robert Braisse-Neuve had intended
that his men should rush the main entrances, and if that were
accomplished without serious loss of life, he had little doubt
that the affair would be all over in a few minutes. But here,
owing mainly to the stubborn valour of Little John, his cal-
culation went far astray. For every portal into the castle was
strongly held, at the main entrance into the keep, Friar Tuck,
with his priestly frock tucked up under his girdle, doing deadly

work with a crab-tree cudgel upon the heads of the Norman pikemen. Moreover, it was impossible for the attackers to advance to within striking distance without being assailed by a veritable hail of well-aimed arrows from the ramparts and the top of the tower. And there were English archers there, famed for their skill from Nottingham to York, who were not to be despised. Though Robin himself may have been the master of them all, there were others who could give near as good an account of themselves.

The Wolf, taking no active part in the combat himself, remained seated on his horse, back by the palisade, whence with a few of the Sheriff's men and his own squires and attendants, he viewed with mingled astonishment and wrath the futility of Norman swords and pikes against English arrows. Yet his sharp and crafty eyes missed nothing. He saw that the lower end of the banqueting-hall was undefended, since the narrow windows were high, and he had come without scaling-ladders. Therefore, when the sun had set behind the tree-tops and it was already growing dark, he gave orders to his torchmen to advance under cover of an undulation in the ground.

"I burn the place out as I would a wasps' nest!" he declared. "Once that pile's a smouldering ruin, we have them at our mercy; and then, since they have followed insult with defiance, ye may leave not one of them alive."

No doubt the sight of so many of his soldiers and the Sheriff's trained men lying lifeless on the ground, and the repeated shouts of "Saint George for England!" that were echoed back from the surrounding woods, infuriated the baron beyond measure, and never had the Wolf been in a more savage mood than then. When one lighted flambeau after another shot like so many fiery vampire-bats through the unglazed windows of the great hall of Newstead, he shouted in exultation; for he knew then that the day was already his.

The floor of the hall was of trodden lime and mud, but in the Norman fashion had been amply strewn with rushes. The walls, too, were half-timbered, but the greatest danger of all was the roof which was of thatch, as in ancient Saxon times. Many of the torches were caught upon the beams and rafters, whence the burning pitch dropped as golden rain upon the dried rushes that were soon ablaze, whilst tongues of fire leapt upward, seized upon the thatch, and spread suddenly into a blaze that ran with the wind like the coming of a wave.

Robin, at the top of the keep, saw at a glance that all was lost, that Newstead was no more. He had several of his best men with him: Will Stutely, David of Doncaster, and Sir Allen-a-Dale; and between them they had wrought no mean havoc on the Normans. But, seeing that if they remained where they were they would be surrounded by a furnace, Robin reluctantly ordered a retreat.

In the main entrance hall at the foot of the tower he met Will Scarlock, Friar Tuck and others who had already beaten back the main attack under the command of the vain knight, Sir Geoffrey. Realising that they must find some way of escape, or they would all be caught like so many rats, Robin told Scarlock to take half a dozen men, leave the castle by the postern to the south, and beat down the outer palisade that they might thereby make good their escape into the forest.

That done, his next thoughts were for his father and his sister, neither of whom he had seen since this dastardly and treacherous assault had broken up the banquet. Someone declared that he had seen the thane at the head of the steps that led to the rampart which connected the keep with the blazing banquet-hall. Thither Robin instantly repaired, leaving Allen-a-Dale to go in search of Marian, concerning whose safety the knightly bard was in considerable anxiety; and, indeed, he had every reason to be apprehensive; for, taking advantage of the confusion caused by the fire, the Normans had already broken their way into the old Saxon castle. Also, Allen, who had been looking forward to a nuptial feast in the very room that was now a sheet of flame, knew of the designs of Sir Stephen de Froy whom—having recovered from the knock-out blow he had received at the hands of Little John—he had seen more than once in the forefront of the fighting.

As for Marian, at the very first alarm, she had hastened to her bower in what was called the Athelstane Tower, because the great and warlike Saxon king had once lodged there for a month; but she had not done so because she shrank from any peril. Maid Marian, despite her beauty, was made of sterner stuff than that. She had seen at a glance that, that day, there was man's work for her to do, and she preferred to do it in a leathern jerkin and buckskin leggings, instead of with fair plaited hair hanging upon soft and silken shoulders. Hence, despite the entreaties of her tiring-maid, she had changed her clothes, caught up her hair, and armed herself with both sword and long-bow. Meeting at the foot of the stairs one of her father's household—Gilbert—she had asked of him what part of the battlements she could render most assistance.

Gilbert's answer had been unfortunate, though he had spoken in the best of faith. He had told her that Stephen Pettifer and others were hard pressed at the eastern gate; and there the Maid was, in the very thick of the fighting, when fire broke out in the hall. Failing to find her in the Athelstane Tower, Allen-a-Dale, distraught for the safety of his true-love, had been cut off in the inner courtyard by de Froy, at the head of a troop of Norman knights and men-at-arms. Finding Pettifer wounded and hearing the news from him that the Maid had been already captured, sword in hand and borne away by force, he was for flinging himself to his death upon the points of Norman pikes, had those with him not restrained him by force.

In the meantime, Robin had witnessed an even greater tragedy than the kidnapping of his beloved sister or the destruction of the home of his ancestors. Alfred of Sherwood, whose forebears had been earls at Newstead before ever a Norman set foot on English soil, rather than desert the home of his fathers threw himself into the very thick of the fray, sword in hand, his object being to close with the Baron of Normanton himself, who had entered afoot by way of the abandoned keep.

It was twilight now, and the red flames illumined the grim and tragic scene. Many of the thane's household had fallen; the roof of the great hall had fallen in, and the walls on either side were crumbling. Snatching a cross-bow from one of his men, Robert the Wolf then and there did a deed that was the next thing to murder, though he thereby fulfilled the oath that he had sworn. The thane was without armour; he had fought throughout in the same short Saxon coat that he had worn at the festive board; and he now faced a score of Norman men-at-arms who had penned him in against the outer wall that the fire had not yet touched, when Braisse-Neuve, taking careful aim, smote him with an arrow through the heart.

Robin, with Stutely, David and others, witnessed this dastardly crime from the opposite side of the court, and like Allen-a-Dale he was for hurling himself to his death, when Friar Tuck grasped him roughly by an arm.

"A truce to such madman's folly, Robin!" he panted. "How can one death avenge another? Remember, though Newstead now perishes in hell's fire itself, thou art still heir to a thanedom that stands for Merry England!"

"And my father—dead!" moaned Robin. "My father's home in flames!"

"May not Sherwood prove a safer home than Newstead?" the good fat friar choked. "To the greenwood, lad! To a man we stand by thee, whatever fate befall us, and in the forest that thou knowest already as well as the palm of thy hand, we may yet defy these Norman scavengers!"

Robin, for a moment, stood like a man transfigured and transformed—mute and motionless. Then, upon a sudden, he raised both his longbow and a shout.

"Aye!" he cried. "To the greenwood! There will I play the wolf myself, and there will I prove that I have cleaner, sharper teeth than yonder murderer and traitor!"

CHAPTER FOUR

ROBIN RESCUES LITTLE JOHN

"To the greenwood!"

The cry was immediately taken up by all who were gathered around Robin of Sherwood that fateful evening when with their faces illuminated by the flames of Newstead, they stood on the margin of the great forest that in those days extended from the north of Nottingham through Mansfield to the valley of the Yorkshire Don. It was the turning point of Robin's life, though he never knew it then; the tragedy that made a law-abiding Saxon thane an outlaw whose name has survived through centuries, whose praises have been sung in many a ballad, and whose prowess and chivalry have been the theme of many a May Day masque and revel.

For a moment, that evening, before his life of lawless chivalry began, he stood there, stricken with distress, like a man in a daze, who could not at first realise the calamity that had so suddenly befallen him; and then turning slowly and sorrowfully from the conflagration of his home, the funeral pyre of the father he had so dearly loved, then and there he made a silent vow that thenceforward he would despoil the Norman, Church and State, to the advantage of those who were impoverished and oppressed. Though of noble Saxon birth himself, he would seek his friends not only among the staunch English yeomen who stood around him—men like Stutely, Much, Arthur-a-Bland, and all the rest of them—but the beggars, palmers and peddlars who tramped the King's highroad, to rest weary limbs at night under the greenwood tree.

"For I now be poor as such as they," he declared; "but so long as we have good yew bows and the King's deer roam in Sherwood, we may live as well as any bishop, prince or baron; and if by chance we overstep the mark in our transgressions, have we not here the good friar to shrive us of our sins?"

"Then let Friar Tuck shrive me now for the knavish thief I be!" cried little Much, who was grinning from ear to ear. "Worthy friar, I make my humble confession here and now, for Will Stutely and I have stolen the treasure-chest of New-stead, though to make due amends he and I be willing to hand it over and all that it contains to Master Robin."

Assisted by Stutely, he now dragged forward a studded oaken chest that was so heavy with gold and silver coins that it was as much as they could do to lift.

Robin started in astonishment, and then his fair bearded face broke into a smile.

"Where found ye this?" he demanded, in a tone of mock severity.

"Where else but in my lord's bed-chamber, where it hath rested these twenty years to my certain knowledge. Though locked it be, Will and I bethought us 'twere better in the greenwood with its rightful owner than serving to swell stuffed Norman purses or melted in the flames."

Robin, with a laugh clapped the little miller on the back.

"Thou hast done right well, Much!" he cried. "And not many moons shall pass before we make More of Much, if I am not mistaken! As for the friar, he can save his shriving. All that concerns me is that I have money enough now to enter my green domain with some show and circumstance. What say ye, comrades, with a horn at my belt, and at my back a goodly company of foresters all clothed in Lincoln green, can mitred priests, sheriff's officers or Norman men-at-arms say me nay?"

His voice was drowned in a shout of applause. Robin held up a hand, commanding silence, for he had not yet spoken all he had to say.

"Since my father lies foully slain and my inheritance be gone," he said, "I may never now be thane of Newstead, but know me henceforward as Robin Hood, since, being too well known by sight, I must wear a hood whenever I go abroad in public places, though free of the greenwood I may be rich as any king."

By this time, on the other side of the castle, the Normans seemed to be withdrawing from the burning building in the growing darkness; and it was at this juncture that Sir Allen-a-Dale came forward, pale of face, and clutched Robin by the arm.

"Marian!" he cried, with a note of despair in his voice. "Robin, hast forgotten her—thy sister? De Froy hath seized her, and you know full well that he hath sworn to wed her, whether she will or no. She is now a prisoner in Norman hands; and this night she will lie at Normanton—a dove in an eagle's nest! I did all I could to save her."

"Marian!" Robin gasped, for this was the first time he had heard that his sister had been stolen. "But take courage, Allen! Though we be not yet strong enough to storm Normanton Castle, there be always ways and means that I may yet devise."

It was Will Scarlock who was the next to speak.

"Were archery of avail against stone walls," he said, "we

should have naught to fear and would bait the Wolf in his lair. Robin, if I am proud of being thy kinsman, I am prouder still that I am cousin to the finest bowman in all England. There may be those among us who may prove thy equal at quarter-staff or sword-play, but no man yet ever lived who was thy master with the longbow. Yet, Robin, not one of us be weaklings; and there are those of our company, such as Much and Little John, who are archers well worthy to be matched against thee— I speak not of myself. Therefore what have we to fear from Norman swords and lances. I wager that within a month thou wilt have two hundred man at thy back—nay, a hundred more than that—all of whom will be sworn to avenge thy murdered father and make thee king of Sherwood."

During this speech Robin had remained thoughtful, having caught swiftly at his beard, as if a sudden doubt had seized upon his mind; and when he spoke, it was in a low soft voice, as if to himself.

"Little John!" he repeated. "Little John! Forsooth, I have not clapped eyes upon him since the friar gave warning of the attack! Where is he now, the staunch companion of my boy-hood, the man who without slight or discourtesy to the true good friends who stand around me—I hold my comrade and the most faithful of friends?"

It was Friar Tuck who made answer.

"Alas!" said he. "*Requiescat in pace!*" And here he crossed himself. "Thy true friend, Sir Robin, is no more. It cannot well be otherwise. Hast forgotten that he, ever faithful to his office, stood warder at the gate. Thence he gave the alarm that I myself heard with my own ears, after which who can doubt that he was smitten down by yonder Norman traitors. What more can we do now than mourn the loss of a good man and true?"

A moment elapsed before Robin answered. Again he was like one in a daze.

"Dead!" he murmured. And then with rising emphasis: "Dead? Nay, I'll not believe it! Is there one here," he asked, "who hath seen him dead? I'll not believe that any Norman hound could lay low so fine a man!"

There was a pause before Friar Tuck again ventured a

suggestion, which from the expression on his kindly, heated countenance he was more than loth to make.

"If he be not dead," he asked, "how else could the Wolf and his men have passed through the palisade."

Robin hesitated no longer. His mind was already made up; and he was a man, as we shall see, with whom action followed close upon the heels of thought.

"Listen," said he, addressing the company in general. "Ye all know well the great oak in the glade by Holling Well. Then let that be our trysting-place. Hasten thither, everyone of you, and expect to see me when ye do. There be the first order I give you in the greenwood, and I think the more of him who obeys me without question." And with that he was gone.

It will be remembered that Robert the Wolf and his Normans had attacked the Saxon tower from the north, since on that side lay all the main entrances into the castle—except the postern to the south—and the only gateway through the outer palisade. Having accomplished his fell purpose and avenged the insult that had been paid by the thane, Braisse-Neuve ordered his men to retire by the way they had come. Sir Stephen de Froy also was anxious to make tracks back to Derby with what dispatch he might, for the baron had made him a solemn promise that he would house Marian at Normanton, until such time as the knight and the maid could be married in accordance with the law and with the sanction of the Church.

For that purpose, at de Froy's request, my lord Bishop of Hereford himself had come to York; and even prior to the attack on Newstead Tower, the banns had been put up at Dale Abbey.

For the nonce, having ordered his men to scatter through the forest, to meet at an appointed place, Robin, bow in hand and sword at belt, worked his way round to the other side of the burning castle, keeping well in the shadow of the trees. No man ever had a heavier heart than he. There were those among his band, such as Will Scarlock and Allen-a-Dale, who were of more noble birth; there was even one man of greater strength—to wit, Arthur-a-Bland, the tanner—though he had neither Little John's great stature nor mastery with the bow; but there was no man among them all whom Robin loved the better, nor any man who loved him more, as we have said, as a great dog loves his master.

Of the banqueting-hall naught remained, but a heap of smouldering ruins, when Robin gained the front of the demolished building. He was still within the enclosure, though he moved stealthily and cautiously along the palisade, in order to keep out of the light of the fire.

All the time he was moving nearer and nearer to the gate, where he had little doubt that he would find the lifeless body of his friend. The stables, he noticed with satisfaction, that stood apart from the main buildings, had not been touched by the fire; and there his father had kept some score of horses which the Normans had overlooked. So much the better, Robin thought. He and some of his men could return upon the morrow, and if there was little that could be salvaged from the fire, they at least would not want for steeds to ride.

Here, at any rate, was one small comforting reflection; and scarce had the thought come into his mind than a cross-bow arrow came singing past his ear, like a bee upon the wing, to bury itself deep in the wooden palisade. His moving figure had been seen in the glowing reflection of the fire, and one glance was enough to tell him that he had at least a score of Norman men-at-arms against him.

Many a man would have turned back then and there, for it seemed that he was bent upon a fool's errand, since he had no reason to doubt that Little John was already dead. But it was Robin's wont never to set forth upon an enterprise and not carry the matter through, for better or for worse. He had at his belt a quiver full of arrows, and the twang of the bow-string was sweet in his ears as the strings of Allen's harp. Still creeping forward, he picked the Normans off one after the other, each man dropping in his tracks so suddenly and in such quick succession that those who were left thought it wiser to look to their own safety.

When Robin himself reached the gate, there were still a dozen men-at-arms within the palisade; and when the first of these went down like a stone with an arrow through his heart, the others thought it best to keep their distance; and this gave Robin all the time he needed.

For there the tall stalwart form of Little John lay prone upon the ground. Not only was there a great bleeding gash on the side of his head, where Sir Geoffrey's axe had struck him, but, with his broken quarter-staff beside him, his arms were outstretched and he had been trampled underfoot, so that his leather jerkin was all besmirched with mire.

Robin, as he knew, had but a few seconds in which to act. Bending down, he felt for his friend's heart; and it was as if his own heart gave a bound when he discovered that Little John, though quite insensible, was still alive.

To hoist a man of such great weight upon a shoulder was naught to Robin of Sherwood; and then, instead of trying to get back to the place where he had left his friends, he passed through the gateway into the forest, turned to the right, to be lost in a second in the darkness under the trees; and an hour later with Little John he had joined Will Stutely and the others by the great oak at Holling Well, which for many years to come was to be his home in the greenwood.

CHAPTER FIVE

MAID MARIAN AND BEATRICE

ROBERT THE WOLF was well content with his day's work at Newstead. Among the most powerful barons in the country, he was second to none in guile. For years now, during the latter half of the reign of King Henry the Second, England had seen naught but lawlessness, disorder and insurrection. Even the King's sons had revolted against him; and Richard, when he came to the throne, had his work cut out to restore order in Normandy and Britain, instead of which he embarked upon a crusade against the Saracen Turks—which had no better result than patched-up truce with Saladin and a bitter quarrel with the King of France.

As King of England, his place was in the country he was

supposed to rule, whence without difficulty he could have guarded his domains in both Anjou and Normandy. But, leaving William of Longchamp, Bishop of Ely—whom he had no special reason to trust—in temporary charge of Britain, he took with him to the Holy Land the majority of the knights and barons upon whose loyalty he could rely—and thus was the way paved for a revolt at the head of which was Prince John, the King's younger brother.

Of John himself, the less said the better. Though he had been his father's favourite son, one cannot find in his character a single redeeming feature. At that time, the Angevin dominion, over which King Richard held uncertain sway, extended from the Tweed to the Pyrenees, and it required a far wiser head than his, even if he had remained in London, to maintain law and order in all the shires of England and the whole of western France. Small wonder, therefore, that during his prolonged absence of four years the more powerful of his subjects, none of whom were over-burdened with scruples, made up their minds to make the best of the opportunity and thereby increase both their influence and estates!

Not least among these disloyal revolting barons was Robert the Wolf, Baron of Normanton and Hautbray, who, like the others, saw in John a weak and cowardly overlord. The Prince was flattered by their false oaths of fealty; and though he feared his warrior brother as a cat fears a dog, King Richard, for the nonce, was more than two thousand miles away. Besides, news in those days travelled but slowly, and it seemed they had time in plenty to place John upon the throne.

In the midlands Robert the Wolf had made his plans both secretly and wisely. He had enlisted the services of the body of the Knights Templar, many of whom had returned from the Holy Land in the disfavour of the King, among whom was him whom we have called the vain knight, Sir Geoffrey Malpert. Sir Geoffrey had other reasons for joining the rebellion, beyond the fact that Cœur-de-lion had cursed him for a popinjay outside the walls of Jaffa, for he had an eye on the main chance and Braisse-Neuve's daughter, the Lady Beatrice of Normanton. Apart from the fact that the Templar believed himself to be irresistible where the fair sex was concerned, and the lady in question was admitted to be one of the greatest beauties in the land, he could scarce fail to see that such an alliance would profit him exceedingly, especially if Prince John came to the throne.

Of greater service to the Wolf in his revolt against the King than a mailed cox-comb like Sir Geoffrey was Sir Stephen de Froy, who had inherited a vast estate in Barnesdale. For here was a knight who had more than once been acclaimed champion in the lists and who moreover had a following of near six hundred squires, men-at-arms, archers and Saxon freemen and serfs. But a small company of these was necessary to assist the baron in the storming of Newstead Tower; but Braisse-Neuve had bigger ambitions for the future than the death of a defiant Saxon franklin, and if all Sir Stephen needed as a reward was the fair Maid Marian of Sherwood, then he was welcome to take her, if he could, so far as Robert the Wolf was concerned. All the baron agreed to do was to house the Saxon damsel in Normanton Castle, until such time as they could be wed in Dale Abbey by the bishop—for Sir Stephen had a mind to be married in a style that befitted his rank and reputation, and if the ceremony took place upon his own estate with all due pomp and circumstance, it would impress the country folk and—for also he believed—assure him of the allegiance of his many Saxon vassals, since a knight so famed and valiant should have condescended to take a Saxon bride.

But that was not the only mistake he made in his ruthless calculations, for he soon found that Marian had inherited her father's spirit and resolution. Though the next thing to a prisoner at Normanton, she refused even to see him, and when he did force himself upon her presence, his pleadings were greeted with contempt and his threats with a defiance such as he had never encountered in either the lists or upon the field of battle.

Moreover, to his chagrin and surprise, he learnt that at Normanton Marian had found an unexpected ally in the Lady Beatrice. For the dark Norman beauty, who had Gascon blood in her veins, loved the fair and upright Saxon maid the very moment she set eyes on her; and if Marian found a prison awaiting her on the hill-top by Derby, she also found a sister. Indeed, more than once did Beatrice try to plead Marian's cause with her father. As for herself, she said, she would rather be wed to a parrot than Sir Geoffrey, since he could do naught but imitate the high talk of bolder and stronger knights than he could ever hope to be. Whereas de Froy, for all his chivalry and knighthood, was no better than a common footpad, since he would steal a noble Saxon maiden as he might filch a purse upon the highroad.

At such talk as this Braisse-Neuve would but shrug his shoulders and show his wolf-like grin. He knew that his daughter had inherited something of his own spirit and tenacity of purpose, if all her good looks had come from the mother who had died when she was a child.

"Concerning thine own affairs," he snapped at her, "thou art free to choose according to thy pleasure."

"And that I will," she took him up. "Nor will I be pleased to choose until I find a proper man."

"A man of birth befitting to thy rank," he answered; "and if we can plant our fickle ranting John safely on the throne, there will be no nobleman in England who may not count himself fortunate if he can win thee. But de Froy be another matter, and no concern of ours. Let it be enough for you to know that he is valuable to me, and no franklin's wench shall stand between Robert Braisse-Neuve and his purpose. Therefore understand once and for all, my hussy, I'll brook no further interference! If the stubborn maid will not go to Dale of her own free will she goeth there by mine; and thou canst tell her that from me."

"It is no better than a crime!" Beatrice cried, indignantly, though tears were welling in her eyes.

At that, in a temper, he flung out of the room; and it was with a heavy heart that Beatrice went back to Maid Marian in her bower.

"There is no hope for it!" she said, sinking into a chair, where she buried her face in her hands, her whole frame shaken by sobs.

Marian went to her at once. She was pale and her lips tight pressed, but otherwise she seemed the master of her feelings.

Placing an arm around her friend's neck, she laid her cheek to hers.

"There is always hope," she whispered. "I have a brother of the name of Robin, and it is Allen whom I love. I know, too, that they have men at their backs with even stouter hearts than any who man these castle walls; and I know full well that they will by now have heard of my distress."

"But what can they do?" asked Beatrice, brushing aside her tears. "Normanton hath walls of iron. Even Cœur-de-lion himself could not free thee."

"Nevertheless, if there be a way, Robin will find it," Maid Marian answered. "And therefore I yet hope, though you may think me foolish."

CHAPTER SIX

DALE ABBEY

IT TOOK Robin but a few days to found his home in the forest by the great oak of Holling Well that, it was said, had been growing when the Saxons first came to England; but it would take more than a few pages to tell how he organised his band, dug caverns under the earth where he might store his provender and treasure, established look-out posts from Nottingham to Sheffield, and trysting-places where his men might gather by appointment over all the country that lies between the Trent, the Derwent and the Don.

Throughout the many months that followed, as the uncrowned king of Sherwood Forest, he was greater than any thane of Newstead; and it was not long before his fame had spread throughout all England. And never was his name mentioned, without a note of pride in his exploits and his deeds. Robber and outlaw he may have been proclaimed, but it was the way he went about his unlawful business, robbing the wealthy to enrich the poor, that made men look upon him as more patriot than brigand.

And more than that, there was not a dishonest cutpurse or a pilfering marauder home from the Holy wars who wanted a safe and easy way of living who did not seek to join his band. Robin Hood would have none of them. Though he plundered the Church of its ill-gotten gains, though he killed the King's deer, baited the Sheriff, and waylaid both baron and knight upon the woodland tracks, he counted himself and his merry men as honest; and moreover, no man would he admit into his company who had not first proved himself an archer, a swordsman or a master at either quarter-staff or cudgel-play.

One need scarcely say that it took Little John but a few days to recover from the knock-out blow he had received from Sir Geoffrey at the gate in the palisade; and during that brief time Robin Hood had not been idle. News had been brought to him that his sister was being held a prisoner at Normanton, until such time as she might be married to Sir Stephen, according to the established rites and with the sanction of the Church, howbeit against her will. And this Robin took to heart as an affront upon his family and a crime little short of the deliberate murder of his father. And even if that had not been so with him, Sir Allen-a-Dale would have given him but little rest. The minstrel may have loved his harp better than the sword he carried at his waist, but, when pressed to it, he could handle either with equal skill and art. Indeed, to rescue his betrothed, he would have forced an entrance into the castle at Normanton itself—and there, as like as not, he would have met his death.

But Robin had a wiser head than he; and he knew that he could never hope to snatch the maid from such a fortress. Accordingly he sent Much into Derby, disguised as a palmer from the Holy Land, and thus advised his sister that she had no need to despair so long as he was alive and had strength to bend a bow.

Nor was the Miller the only one that during those anxious days of waiting played the spy. Martin, Arthur-a-Bland and David, who hailed from Doncaster, all entered the town, where they listened to the gossips in the market-place, whither the news had leaked out from behind the gaunt and silent castle walls. Of the circumstance that the Saxon maid in the castle

was in no mind to wed the Norman knight they knew nothing;
but that there was to be a grand procession, a cavalcade of
knights, nobles and esquires, all clothed in costly raiment,
from Derby to Dale Abbey was good enough for them. And,
also, though in a very different sense, it was good enough for
Robin.

And truly, when the great day came, the good citizens of
Derby were in no way disappointed. Heralds sounded a fanfare
of trumpets as the cortège issued from the drawbridge, headed
by a body of knights. But it was the bride herself to whom all
the eyes of the populace—especially the women—were immediately attracted. Maid Marian was mounted on a white palfrey
that was gorgeously caparisoned. Her fair hair was arranged in
ringlets, but devoid of jewels. Indeed she wore no ornaments,
but a heavy golden necklet and bracelets round her arms.
Beneath the scarlet woollen robe that depended from her
shoulders were a gown and kirtle of pure white and of the very
finest silk. But what amazed the crowd more than anything else
was that her bridal veil was thrown back, as if she feared not
who might see that her face was as white as her dress. She
neither smiled nor moved a muscle of her soft, even features,
and her blue eyes seemed to gaze and see nothing, though there
was a strange light in them of keen, yet suppressed, expect-
ancy.

The Lady Beatrice of Normanton rode beside her; and there
was not one among the crowd that thronged Derby streets
that early morning who did not note, by the expression on her
face, for her dark brows were knit, and more than once she
was seen to bite her nether lip.

The baron himself brought up the rear of the cavalcade,
attended by numerous knights and esquires. The townsfolk
had some cause to know the Wolf both by sight and reputation,
and seldom had he appeared to them in a more ill mood than
then. When the people would have cheered—though few
could have given any reason why they should—his very scowl
as he passed chilled them into silence.

In the meantime, another, and very much smaller, party
was riding south from Barnesdale through the northern part
of Sherwood Forest and the heather land round Mansfield.

Sir Stephen de Froy, with a few chosen friends and such attendants as in those days were thought necessary for every man of rank, rode to Dale Abbey with greater speed than was needful. Like the knights in Braisse-Neuve's cavalcade, they carried no arms, save swords; and as upon the road they used their gilded spurs more often than their tongues, it was a certain thing that they must have long to wait for both Braisse-Neuve and the Bishop.

On arrival at the Abbey, more than an hour before his time, he found to his surprise that he was not the first by any means; for the road was crowded with country folk, many of whom he could not remember ever to have seen before, though the church stood upon his own estate. There was a brawny tanner there, a potter, a tall swine-herd, and a little miller whose jerkin was snow-white with flour. Scarce a glance he gave them —for he counted them as so many Saxon sheep, beneath the contempt of a courtly Norman knight—but flung into the Abbey, where, seating himself near the south transcept, he drummed with his fingers on a knee, tapped his toes on the hard stone floor, and worked himself into a very frenzy of impatience.

In due time—since all things come at last to him who waits— the Prior himself deigned to put in an appearance. With hood and mantle of the very finest cloth that ever came out of Flanders, a gold necklet beneath his double chins, and fat fingers that were squeezed in gems, he clearly did not think it necessary for so high a dignitary to observe the rigid regulations of the Cistercian order to which he belonged. Indeed, no prosperous merchant in London town itself could have looked better fed or better cared for, nor could any Norman baron—even Robert Braisse-Neuve himself—have counted himself of greater importance, judging by the way the Prior treated his attendant priests.

Yet no man could have shown himself more menial and abject when my lord Bishop of Hereford, thin and gaunt, with a hooked nose like a vulture and a pate as bald, came stalking through the vestry door. But, though the Bishop had the appearance of a man who had denied himself all wordly joys and comforts in the service of the Church, he was well known to be both miserly and mean, though he had made a fortune out of usury. For no one knew better than he that money could buy power; and, if John came to the throne, he aimed at being both Papal Legate and Lord Justiciar of all England.

By this time, too, Master Hamnett, the Sheriff of Nottingham, had entered the abbey with his good and comfortable spouse, who was all agog to see so fine a wedding. So, on the arrival of the cavalcade from Derby, there was not a pew nor seat in the nave or aisles that was not filled; for the vacant places at the back had been taken by the common people who had now thronged into the church. Several of these packed the gallery at the western end; and among those who were seated there were those strangers we have already mentioned: the potter, the tanner, and the little miller whose coat was white with flour.

Thus the service began with all due sanctity and ceremony, then the pale unwilling bride was led to the chancel by the Baron of Normanton and Hautbray; and it was at that very moment that a most strange and ill-assorted couple thrust themselves through the crowd at the porch, to find seats immediately on either side of the central passage that led from the lectern to the font. For one was a portly friar with the hempen cord around his stomach so tight upon his brown rough cassock that he had to loosen it now and again for comfort and the other was an old woman, hooded and bent double, who might have been a witch.

Only those who were seated near at hand were curious to know who the old hag might be, for by reason of the hood that covered her lowered head they could not see her face. However, as to that, they were kept not long in doubt, for the service was no more than begun that the old woman stepped forth into the middle of the nave, straighted her crooked back, and cried out in a man's voice:

"I hereby forbid this marriage as a sin against both God, the Church and justice! Another word from thee, my lord bishop, and thou shalt render an account of thy usuries in Heaven!"

The Bishop gasped. The Prior dropped the holy book he was holding in his hand. Those in front turned their heads, aghast and affronted; whilst those at the back stood on tiptoe, to see the cause of such commotion. One or two of the knights even grasped the handles of their swords, and among these was de Froy himself.

It was the Bishop who was the first to find his voice.

"Who is this crone?" he cried, his voice trembling with rage. "Who hath dared profane this holy place?"

"Which be the greater profanity," the other rapidly demanded: "to force a marriage on an unwilling maid who has been snared like a bird in a gin, or to defy openly a bunch of traitors who would use God's name to serve their crooked ends?"

"Seize the witch!" the Bishop ordered. "Take her forth from the church, and let her be held a prisoner without, until such time as we can deal with her as she deserves!"

Several turned to obey the command, when upon a sudden the witch's hood and mantle were flung upon the floor; and there stood in the very centre of them all one, in the full strength of early manhood, who had shaved off his beard and who was clothed in Lincoln green. Moreover, he bent a great bow in his hands, and the cloth-yard shaft was directed straight at the Bishop's heart.

As for that grim and worldly cleric, in his anger he had advanced several steps down the chancel; but he now stopped stone-dead, with his eyes fixed upon the intruder.

"Art mad?" he cried. "Who be this knave who has dared, in God's edifice itself, to fling defiance at the Church?"

The answer came in a voice that rang from transcept to transcept, from the western gallery to the altar.

"Robin Hood! That be the name by which every one of ye will soon learn to know me. And look well around, my lords spiritual and temporal, before ye think to do anything rash! There be not a boastful knight or sleek grovelling priest among the lot of ye who is not a marked man, and of those who hold ye pinned to where ye stand, there is not an archer who could fail to find his mark."

A silence fell upon that splended gathering that was like a sudden suspension of the universe itself, until several women shrieked, and there were one or two who even fainted. For many moments no one spoke, and none dared move aught save their heads, to see if in very truth they stood in danger of their lives.

They had no need to look long; nor could any sight have been less to their liking or more to the dishonour of gallant knights who had ranked themselves as champions. For the whole church was crowded with men in Lincoln green; standing up upon the pews, they were ranged about the walls of both aisles; whereas the gallery was naught else but a veritable phalanx of bowmen, all of whom were covering with their arrows every man of import who stood gasping and helpless in the nave. And among these latter were all the finest archers in Robin's band: Much and Little John, Will Stutely and Will Scarlock, and the rest of them—all save Allen-a-Dale who had appeared from somewhere at the back of the church and now stood close at Robin's elbow. In a trice they had cast aside their various disguises; as at a stroke from a wizard's wand, potter, mendicant and miller had become the merry men of the greenwood. It was Robin Hood, and the Bishop of Hereford no longer, who was there to see that Maid Marian was married.

And it was Robin, too, who now spoke again. Leaving the Bishop to be marked by Allen, he had directed the shaft in his bent bow at the chest of Robert Braisse-Neuve.

"Were this not a sacred edifice," said he, "I would slay thee here and now as the murderer of my father, as I would put to a quick death without thought or pity any other wolf! As it is, I give thee leave to depart with such of thine own attendants as care to follow thee. If thou resist, thy blood be on thine own head; and by the same token, I hereby give fair warning to ye all: if so much as a sword be drawn an inch from its sheath, though this be God's own house and I be a man of honour, the man who tries to draw falls dead!"

Another brief and breathless silence greeted this speech, during which the baron was seen to carry a hand to his chin and stand for a moment thinking.

Braisse-Neuve felt as if his heart was a blazing furnace. He cared naught for the Bishop or the Prior; but that he, one of the most powerful barons in the country, and more feared than any, should be so caught off his guard and openly defied, was more than he could swallow. The fact that he had been denounced as a murderer before the whole congregation there assembled meant less to him than an insult from a Saxon franklin's whelp that he would not brook from Cœur-de-lion himself.

Yet he had ever been one who could think both clearly and quickly in moments of emergency; and it now occurred to him that, if he pretended to obey and forthwith left the church with what dignity he might, he had attendants and soldiers outside who had been left in charge of the horses. Therefore his chagrin and disgust may be better imagined than described when, on coming forth of the porch with his sword still unsheathed, he found that another company of green-clad bowmen had not only held up his serving-men and pages, but had disarmed, and even robbed the lot of them.

Fuming with rage and grinding his teeth, he had no option therefore but to fling himself swearing into the saddle on his horse; and it is a fact that, that evening, the Baron of Normanton and Hautbray rode back to his castle alone. And when he got there, so the rumour goes, he was like a savage beast in a cage; for all night long, from dusk to daybreak, he paced his room, vowing that no vengeance could be more swift or terrible than that which he would bring down upon the head of Robin Hood.

CHAPTER SEVEN

THE MERRY MEN

IN THE meanwhile, when Robert the Wolf was spurring back to Normanton, venting his wrath upon his luckless steed, a scene was taking place in Dale Abbey which, though the first, was one of Robin's most daring and outrageous exploits.

No sooner was he quit of the baron than he again addressed the Bishop.

"My lord Bishop of Hereford," said he, "since so fine and gallant a congregation be here assembled to witness the holy rites of matrimony, it seemeth to me something of a shame that the ceremony shall not continue. So, if it please your lordship to fulfil your holy office, I warrant my bowmen and I see to it that all here give ear to the service with becoming reverence."

The Bishop, to give him his due, was no craven, and without doubt would have made a better knight than churchman. But not so the Prior, who was quaking in his shoes.

"I am not come hither," his lordship was bold enough to answer, "to carry out my sacred duties under threats from such as thee."

"Sacred!" Robin took him up. "I declare to one and all that this maid was borne away by force, and if there be anything sacred in that, then I never bent a bow. Moreover, my lords and ladies, seeing that she be my sister, I may, perhaps, have leave to speak on her behalf; and that I do, when I say she would rather be wedded to a Saxon serf than yonder haughty knight, to whom thou wouldst sell her like a bauble that he may aid thee and other like traitors in an enterprise against the King."

De Froy, all this time, had stood scowling and impotent beneath the pulpit; but this was more than he could brook. Involuntarily his hand went to the hilt of his sword, and he had half drawn the blade, when Robin told him to beware.

"See well to it, Sir Knight, that you do not force me to spill blood in this holy place! How often thou hast proved a champion in the lists I neither know nor care; but, if thou hast eyes in thy head, thou canst not fail to see that thou art no champion now."

Sir Stephen, after a quick glance around him, and seeing that Robin's was not the only arrow that had marked him as a target, rapped the blade home with a muttered oath.

"Then," said he, "wilt thou give thy sister to me for my bride?"

Robin burst into a laugh.

"Since thou hast proved thou art not blind, I must fain believe thee deaf. Marian will marry the man of her choice, and since she has already chosen well, I am here to see, as I have said, that this day this gay and goodly company beholds a marriage. She would be bound willingly, Sir Knight, in holy wedlock, and not in Norman fetters—and for that no man here can blame her. My Lord Bishop, thou camest hither for a purpose, to make man and maid, husband and wife. Surely such a high church dignitary will not swerve from the path of duty? I understand thou art paid for such business, though such salary may be a pittance compared to what can be made by holding mortgages on poor men's land on behalf of Holy Church?"

The Bishop swallowed the insult, though his gaunt face had turned green with rage.

"I'll have naught to do with this!" he cried. "Sacrilege and outrage such as has never been seen before! I order every person here at once to leave the abbey!"

"So priesthood be as deaf as chivalry!" Robin taunted. "Have I not said we are all here to see a wedding. Good friar," he added, turning to Friar Tuck, "get about the Bishop's business! I doubt me little thou wilt do it as well as he, though he would get the better of thee in a bargain."

Friar Tuck had rolled into the chancel, where he snatched the book out of the Bishop's hands before his lordship was aware of what had happened.

For the first time since the ceremony had been so scandalously and rudely interrupted, the Prior of Dale found his voice, though the probability was that it was sheer fright that drove the breath from his lungs.

"What hedgerow monk be this!" he cried. "Know ye not that I am prior here?"

"Aye," parried Robin, "I know that by the rings upon thy fingers. But, I take it, one priest be as good as any other. And since it takes two parties to made a contract, whether it be a marriage contract or a mortgage—to which my Lord Bishop will doubtless agree—I have here another bridegroom. Right willingly, before you all, I hereby give my sister, Maid Marian of Sherwood, to be wedded to Sir Allen-a-Dale. And now, my honest, friendly friar, get ahead with thy work, since I have already preached the sermon!"

Allen had stepped forward and now stood at Marian's side; and Friar Tuck had read the initial lines of the service, when again the Bishop intervened.

"Be it known to all," he cried, "that this ceremony is against the law of England!"

Friar Tuck looked round at his lordship, and there was certainly none of that deference in the expression of his face that had been exhibited by the Prior.

"How so?" he asked. "Be it against the law for a Saxon knight to take the place of a Norman? *Deo, patriæ, amicis*—by which I mean, my Lord Bishop, having in my youth learned more of Latin than the law, that I here serve God, my country and my friends; and by so doing I can do no harm."

"Yet," the Bishop persisted, "this thing be illegal, since the banns of these two who have now presented themselves to be married have never been cried thrice in this church nor any other."

When all is said and done, the Bishop had by now well proved himself the stubbornest of all of them. He intended, if he could, to prevent the marriage taking place; and if he could do so at the eleventh hour, he knew he would gain favour in the eyes of both Robert Braisse-Neuve and Sir Stephen, who were hand in glove with him at the head of the insurrection against the absent King, as he had been bested in argument with Robin, who was ever as quick with an answer as he was with a shaft in his bow, so now he found his match in Friar Tuck.

"Ho, ho!" exclaimed that jovial holy clerk. "Fool that I were to think a lord bishop could ever be in the wrong! Thrice, dost thou say, should the banns be published? Grammercy, my lord, though I be but a simple friar, I can do a lot better than that. No less than twelve times, and here and now, shall I cry these banns, that Maid Marian and Sir Allen-a-Dale may be as good as four times married."

And thereupon, in a great voice that filled the whole church, even to the rafters, he asked if there were any one among the assembled congregation who knew of any just impediment why these two should not be wedded; and twelve times, as he had said, did he roar at them the prescribed and legal question. And never an answer came from the body of the church—as was natural enough, since many of the knights had by now taken their departure in the same manner as the baron, and of those who remained not a few were grinning. As for the rest, such as the Sheriff, they could do naught but scowl; for Robin's archers in the gallery and aisles were as much in charge of the ceremony as the friar in the chancel.

The legal business thus satisfactorily concluded, according to Friar Tuck's broad and generous views, he continued the service to the end, and thereby making Marian and Allen man and wife; and when they walked together through the porch and came out into the open air, they received a cheer from Robin's men who were there on guard that must have echoed many a mile over hill and dale.

As for Robin, he thus addressed those who remained within the abbey.

"Ye have seen this day a Saxon wedding," he declared, "and I have no mind to let it pass without celebrating such a happening in the olden English fashion. Those who would depart forthwith—and I doubt not there are many—may do so at their leisure; though I warn them there are many and good bowmen without who will obey their orders, if a single sword be unsheathed. As for the rest, if there be any among ye who have a mind to sample a Saxon feast, I invite them to join my merry men in toasting the bride and bridegroom under the greenwood tree."

And a feast, in very truth, it was—the first of many such as Sherwood saw in the days of Robin Hood. For, when the company was assembled in the glade by Holling Well, the board had been already spread with roasted venison, swansmeat and pasties, and every delicacy the store-room underground could provide; and though there was water in the nearby spring that was crystal clear, not a man among them sampled it. For they had every kind of wine, though there was ale for those who liked it—of which number was never the portly friar, who gave the toast of the bride and bridegroom. At the head of the table the friar cracked his jokes, as he lowered cup after cup; and when he was not roaring with his jovial infectious laughter, he was cursing between mouthfuls every Saxon fool who chose to serve a Norman lord.

And after that, they passed an hour or so with bouts of quarter-staff and cudgel-play, at which the friar took a hand.

Laid flat by Little John with a blow from a staff that would have felled an ox, the fat holy clerk got panting to his feet and challenged Robin himself to a wrestling match that ended in Robin being cast neck and crop into the stream that flowed through the glade. This exploit of the friar's was greeted with cheers, in which Robin was the first to join. And thus came it about that throughout the centuries the green-clad foresters were known as Robin's Merry Men.

CHAPTER EIGHT

NOTTINGHAM FAIR

DURING the next few months Sir Robert Braisse-Neuve, in his strong keep at Normanton, was resolved to leave no stone unturned to dig Robin Hood out of his earth in Sherwood Forest. Scarcely a day passed when he did not hear of some new outrage by the outlaw; and it was soon admitted on every hand that it was not safe for any high church dignitary, noble-man or man of wealth to journey unattended by a strong bodyguard upon any of the roads between Nottingham and Barnesdale, especially the western branch of Watling Street that leads to Doncaster and York.

The Wolf was never a man who could accept such an insult as Robin had paid him in Dale Abbey; and his ill mood was by no means mollified by the fact that his daughter now practically ignored him. She spoke to her father only when she must, and even then he had more than once to reprimand her for not keeping a civil tongue in her head. For he considered he had cares enough without family quarrels. In the first place, the insurrection against King Richard was not going as well as it might, and the fault for this was mainly due to Prince John himself. For the baron was one who believed in striking when the iron was hot, and never had the rebel lords and prelates a better chance than then.

For the fact was the Cœur-de-lion, hearing of the great disorder that prevailed in England, made up his mind to return from Palestine and set sail from Jaffa. But misfortune almost immediately befell him, for he fell into the hands of his enemies —of whom he had more than even he could master—and was imprisoned in a German castle, from which escape seemed well-nigh impossible. Had John, on hearing of this misfortune to his brother, been a man of a different kidney, he would have seized the crown by force of arms—and that he might have done without much difficulty or danger, seeing that he had many of the most powerful barons at his back. But, being careless as he was treacherous, and loving luxury more than warfare, he spent his time at masques, tournaments and revels; while Robert Braisse-Neuve chafed, fumed and swore in his great hall at Normanton.

Word had been sent him that the Prince was coming north; and he had already made arrangements to hold a council at Normanton Castle that would be attended by all the rebel lords, including the Grandmaster of the Templars, the Bishop of Hereford and Sir Stephen de Froy. What he hoped to do was to raise an army in the midlands, persuade the fickle treacherous Prince to place himself at its head, and march straight on London, where both the Bishop of Ely and the majority of the citizens were still loyal to the King.

With the cares of such great issues lying heavy on his shoulders, the Wolf yet found time to make plans for the capture of Robin Hood. Since John might arrive in Derby at any moment, he could not spare more than a few of his mounted men-at-arms; but these he readily placed at the disposal of the Sheriff of Nottingham, and scarcely a day passed when his messengers were not riding post-haste between the two midland towns.

In Nottingham, on the other hand, Master Hamnett was no less perplexed. The captain of his guard had long since informed him that it was quite impossible for the King's keepers and rangers in the forest to oppose Robin and his band, which was increasing in numbers every day. On several occasions the Sheriff himself made inroads into the woods with a strong force of archers and men-at-arms, hoping that he might be able to round up the famed outlaw and his men. But it might have been of as much avail to set a flock of sheep to catch a hare. Robin might have fought them, had he willed, but he was in no mind to shed the blood of innocent men at the bidding of the Sheriff and Sir Robert Braisse-Neuve. He preferred therefore to give them the slip, and about this he never found the slightest difficulty. He and his men knew every glade, dale and moor between the Trent and the Don; and though the outlaw had established his secret headquarters at Holling Well, in the southern part of the forest, it was his custom to wander far afield. Whenever the Sheriff marched out of Nottingham with the next thing to a small army, which was obliged to keep to the roads and woodland paths, Robin and his men would break up and scatter, gathering again at some appointed place many miles distant, where they would unburden a fat prior of his jewels or a travelling usurer of his golden zecchins.

The more the Sheriff tried, the more often did he fail even to get a sight of the elusive forester, and the more often and the more heartily would he be cursed by Robert Braisse-Neuve. This afforded so much sport for Robin, who always knew all that was afoot, since the townsfolk of both Nottingham and Derby never failed to keep him posted in the latest gossip. He knew, too, of the plot against the King and that Prince John himself would soon be coming to the midlands; and though he killed the King's deer, he had sworn that he would never raise a hand or bend a bow against any of the King's own men. Even the rangers in Sherwood Forest he counted not as enemies, though they were welcome to catch him if they could.

The Sheriff soon, being a conscientious and simple man, was in the depths of deep despair; for he could neither please the lord of Normanton nor lay hands on Robin Hood. And hearing of this, the bold outlaw decided at once to play a trick on him and fulfil the oath he had sworn.

The design he contemplated meant that he must take into the secret two of his most trusted men; and he pitched upon Little John and Arthur-a-Bland, the tanner, than whom there were none stronger in all his merry company. Cutting off both his long hair and beard, the former donned a suit of scarlet, so fine a raiment indeed that, with a great feather in his cap, he might have been some gallant of the court; and thus attired, he set off to Nottingham, the day before there was to be a fair that all the town would attend, even the Sheriff himself.

As may be imagined, Little John, with his manly limbs and great stature, being dressed so gallantly, caused no small sensation among the maidens of that town, who are reckoned to be the fairest in all England. But the tall forester had no eyes for their soft inviting looks in his direction, for he was concerned with bigger and harder game than arch wenches who were suffering unduly from palpitations of the heart. Arrived at the fair, he elbowed his way through the throng to a booth where he had seen Master Hamnett, the Sheriff, seated with his good wife before a man who looked like a bull and who was challenging all comers to try their skill at quarter-staff against the champion of the midlands.

"I have five gold zecchins here that I got from a Jew in Chester," he proclaimed, in a voice that matched his burly frame, "and that much will I pay to any man among you who will step forth upon the stage and rob me of my title."

This was a prize that the youth and yeomanry of Nottingham thought it worth while to capture to their own advantage and the honour of their town. As for Little John, he resolved to stand back awhile and watch the fun, whilst at the same time he sized up the prowess and the methods of the so-called champion of the midlands.

There were about five challengers who were bested in quick succession, three crying out that they had had enough of it, and the other two being knocked senseless on the stage, much to the amusement of the Sheriff and the good folk of Nottingham.

"And now 'tis time I took a hand," said Little John to himself; "and though I reckon it will be no easy matter, if I cannot well belabour this Tom o'Cudgels, who makes a living at country fairs, then may I never hold a quarter-staff again!"

With these words, he thrust his way through the audience, and stepped forth upon the platform.

"Another sheep for the shearing!" scoffed the champion, rubbing the palm of a hand upon his unshaven protruding chin. "A right proper man in inches, I dispute not that; but methinks, thou art dressed more for a banquet than a bout at quarter-staff!"

"If that be so," Little John replied, "'tis a matter easily put right, though I should advise thee, Master Champion, never judge a man by what he wears. Ye have yet to learn that ye would shear a sheepskin on a wolf."

This gibe so pleased the Sheriff that he chuckled aloud and nudged his good wife in the ribs.

"If he be as quick with a staff as he is with his tongue," said he, "we will see now a pastime worthy of the watching."

"I know not how he will fare in the bout," Mistress Hamnett answered. "That be for a man to judge. All I can say is that never did I see a finer yeoman. Of a surety he comes not from Nottingham, or I would have noticed him before."

The good lady was beaming all over her face, and she could not move her eyes from Little John who now, having doffed his scarlet coat, displayed the muscles on his great arms, which were like strands of whipcord. Clearly Mistress Sheriff had the same eyes in her head as many of the fair maids of Nottingham who were not half her age.

The champion, on the other hand, did not seem so pleased as he had been with either Little John's taunts or his personal appearance. Nor did he feel over confident when his challenger went to a stack of quarter-staffs, and selected one that was to his liking as to weight and balance in the manner of an expert.

"I see," said he, "thou art no novice at this game; but I reckon I can crack thy pate as easily as thou canst crack a joke."

"And if you reckon wrong," the other took him up, "then the joke will be on my side, as well as thy five golden zecchins."

In a few seconds they had set to it, with the crowd all expectant and agog. Shouting wagers at one another, they had a notion they were about to see a combat such as seldom came their way.

Nor were they mistaken, as was apparent from the very start. For the champion opened and pressed home the attack with a skill and violence such as he had not thought it worth his while apparently to exert upon his previous opponents. Oak staff rang on oak as Little John parried one blow after another ; and then, upon a sudden, he got a buffet on a shoulder that would have sent a lesser man reeling across the stage. Indeed, the champion, thinking he had made an opening, swung back his staff to deliver what he thought would be the knock-out blow—instead of which it was he himself who took what he meant to give. For Little John struck for the first and only time, and the swing of his staff was like the stroke of a falcon. The vaunted champion of the midlands received a buffet on the side of his head that sent him senseless to the flooring, where he lay flat upon his face and never moved an inch.

Mistress Hamnett was seen to whisper something in her spouse's ear; and although the Sheriff rose from his seat and held up a hand for silence, several minutes elapsed before the crowd would cease their cheering.

When at last there was silence, it was to Little John that the Sheriff thus addressed himself.

"Never in all my days," he exclaimed, "have I seen such work so swiftly done! I warrant there be few men in England who could stand against thee! By what name, sire, do they call thee and whence came you to Nottingham?"

"Reynold Greenleaf is my name, Sir Sheriff, and I hail from Holderness," Little John replied, acting the part he had been taught by Robin. "But I count myself not much of a hand at quarter-staff, your honour. It can be a game well enough to play, by way of passing the time, with such country lobs as yonder champion, who seems to be coming slowly back to life. Archery is the pastime in which I am reputed to be something near proficient. I make no boast when I say I can shoot a shaft a mile, and more than once I have split a cane at more than a hundred paces."

The Sheriff gasped for breath.

"By Saint Dunstan," he exclaimed, "I verily believe thee! It is for such men as thee that I am combing every hamlet in the shire. Of thy strength and skill at quarter-staff I have seen enough; and if you be the archer that you claim to be, thou wouldst be a match for Robin Hood himself."

"Robin Hood?" repeated Little John, as if he had never heard the name before in his life. "And who be Robin Hood? Bring him here to me, good Master Sheriff, and I wager the five golden coins that I have but now fairly won that he will never out-match Reynold Greenleaf with yew bow and grey goose-shaft."

"Alas," the Sheriff answered, "would that I could bring him hither! But this much can I promise: if thou, Reynold, wilt take service under me, thou shalt fare right well in Nottingham Castle, and for what help you give me in running this arch-knave to earth, thou wilt be handsomely requited."

Little John opened wide his eyes, as if the offer pleased him— as in very truth it did, seeing that he had come to Nottingham Fair for no other purpose.

"Why, be this Robin Hood a knave?" he asked.

"None greater in all England," the Sheriff made answer. "And I am sworn to hang him high on the gallows in this very market-place."

"Then, if that be so," said Little John, stepping down from the stage, "I am thy very man, Sir Sheriff, for all lawless knaves do I most heartily abhor; and right willingly will I take service under thee."

Thus did it come about that this same Reynold Greenleaf took up his quarters in Nottingham Castle, where he wrought that which he was sent to do.

CHAPTER NINE

NOTTINGHAM CASTLE

FROM THE very day on which he took service under the Sheriff, Little John, going by the name of Reynold Greenleaf, made himself thoroughly at home in Nottingham Castle. Being much in the favour of Mistress Hamnett, he was free to go where he listed, and soon made good friends with the cook, who gave him many a tasty dish that was meant for the Sheriff's private table. By reason of his great strength, good looks and merry disposition, he was popular with all the servants, both male and female, as well as the Sheriff's officers and even the head jailer. As for Master Hamnett himself, having seen something of Little John's skill at archery, he would never go a-hunting without him, and swore that, if he had but twenty of such men, he would soon bring Robin Hood to book.

Indeed, there was only one man in the household with whom Reynold Greenleaf was not popular—and that was the most important person of all, after the Sheriff himself. For Master Warren, the castle steward, never had a good word to say for the newcomer, who he seemed to think had somehow usurped the privileges he regarded as his own. The steward himself was a man well above the average height and proportionally broad of shoulder. Vain as a peacock, concerning the high office he held and his personal appearance, he looked upon a finer specimen of manhood than himself in the light of an intruder, and made no secret of the fact that, if he ever caught Master Reynold Greenleaf meddling in matters that were no concern of his, he would soon have him under lock and key in the castle prison.

Little John held his peace and restrained his impatience, knowing full well that his time would shortly come.

For all this he was in almost daily communication with Robin himself and Arthur-a-Bland. Robin was therefore able to get all information he wanted from Little John and to make his plans accordingly. Thus he learnt that on a certain Wednesday it behoved the Sheriff to go a-hunting over Bulwell Heath, on the outskirts of Sherwood Forest; and again nothing could have suited Robin better.

On the morning of the hunt, the Sheriff as usual sent for Little John, for by this time he would do naught without his trusty henchman, Reynold Greenleaf. Little John had dressed in the scarlet suit in which he cut so fine a figure; but, when he presented himself before his master, he looked a sorry sight, indeed. For he was holding the pit of his stomach with both his great hands, whilst at the same time he snorted and grunted like a baited bull.

"'Tis the colic, master!" he avowed. "Blame the cook for a dish of fried eels he gave me yesternight. It is as if a fire consumed my vitals! I cannot even stand upright, much less sit astride a horse."

"A plague on thee and the cook as well!" exclaimed the

Sheriff. "I have notice there are wolves on Bulwell, and am I to go after them without the best archer that I have?"

" 'Tis a wolf that gnaws within me," Little John declared. "Were I to try to bend a bow this day, thou wouldst have the trouble and expense of burying me to-morrow."

And at that he let out another groan; so that Master Hamnett flung away from him in a temper and set off upon his hunting with about a score of men.

And no sooner was the Sheriff at the bottom of the castle hill than he and those with him passed a potter and his mate, who were on their way to sell the cook an earthenware bowl for stewing; and it was about this time, too, that Little John suddenly recovered from his colic. For the potter was none other than Robin Hood, accompanied by Arthur-a-Bland. There were pots, pans and bowls, sure enough, in the cart, but, on this special occasion, they concealed three long yew bows and a like number of cudgels.

The cook was a kind and friendly man, and Little John meant him no harm when he trussed him like a capon, gagged his mouth, and tied him to one of the legs of the kitchen table. As for the scullery wenches, driving them before him like so many panic-striken poults, Master Greenleaf locked the lot of them up in the woodshed, though he never forgot his manners.

"It goeth much against the grain in me," he said, "that the pick of the beauty of all Nottingham should be compelled to consort with wood-lice; but, I promise ye, I'll open the dove-cot when I have finished with the work I have to do."

This done he joined Robin and Arthur at the kitchen door.

"Be all in readiness?" Robin asked. "Then let us about our business as quickly as we may. The steward's the rogue we want. Where can we find him?"

"In the great hall," said Little John. "He hath about a dozen men with him, and they are arranging the tables for the banquet that is to be held after the hunting."

Robin burst into laughter and clapped his comrade on the back.

"Aye, banquet he shall, but never here this evening! Lead the way, John! Arthur and I will follow."

With their longbows in their hands, and at their belts their staves and quivers crammed with arrows, they passed up a flight of stone steps, along a narrow dimly-lighted passage, and thence into the hall, which—as good luck had it—had but a single entrance.

Their sudden appearance was as astonishing as unexpected to all those within the room who were working under orders from Master Warren; but what made the situation a trifle embarrassing, so far as Robin was concerned, was that Mistress Hamnett herself was superintending the operations. A long oaken table stood on the raised platform at the far end of the room, and the serving-men were in the act of setting up several trestle-tables on the lower floor at right angles to the dais, when their work was so rudely interrupted.

"Hold!" Robin shouted. "Ye have all the afternoon before you, whereas I and my two friends have much to do and little time to spare."

Every one in the hall stood as if amazement had turned them all to stone; for in the doorway stood the potter, with his ragged mate on one side of him and the man they had known as Reynold Greenleaf on the other, and all three had their left arms full extended and right arms drawn back, grasping the feathered ends of the shafts that were fixed in the taut angles of their bow-strings.

"What means this?" cried Warren, who was seen to be shaking like a leaf. "To enter here be crime enough, but to bend a bow upon a sheriff's officer is enough to send all three of ye to the gallows!"

"True, indeed!" Robin agreed. "But, before you can eat a hare, you must snare it first. Move an inch, Master Steward, and they can make a stew of thee for all thou wilt be worth!"

Mistress Hamnett clutched her heart and sank down upon a bench. Warren went on, though before he could speak again he had to swallow something in his throat.

"Reynold Greenleaf, I ever knew thee and thy potter friends to be rogues. Dost think that thou canst slay one of us under the Sheriff's very roof-tree and yet escape the gallows?"

"No mere potter would, I warrant," Little John replied. "But my simple potter spins a wheel of his own in Sherwood Forest, and they call him Robin Hood. So now you know,

Warren, where I got my skill in archery. Howbeit, we have come not to bandy words, but to help ourselves to the Sheriff's plate-chest which, I see, you have been considerate enough to bring into the hall."

As he was speaking, Robin had sprung on to a table at the end of the room, whence he seemed to cover every man there with the feathered shaft in his bow.

"There are certain folk," he declared, "whom I like to look upon as sheep, and as such I count every man here. Hence, like sheep, would I like ye closer together, as you were in a pen. Close up, every man of ye, around Master Warren, so that ye may feel like so many sheep beneath a stout oak tree in a thunderstorm, though I give fair warning that at any moment that tree, if I see aught amiss, may be struck by lightning!"

They obeyed, as obedient as the sheep he had called them to the barking of a sheep dog. And in the meantime, Robin, without moving his eyes from the steward, addressed himself to the mistress of the castle.

"What I have said, good dame, can in no way apply to thee, for thou hadst ever a soft place in thy heart for simple potters. Sit there and rest and fear not, for there be naught to fear. And now, John and Arthur, to work! Show these castle rats that they would have to go a long way to find stronger men. But, first, relieve that quaking steward of his keys, for we will need more than one of them before they see the last of us."

Little John and Arthur-a-Bland had slung their bows over their shoulders and now advanced down the room. As the former unhooked the ring of keys from Warren's belt, he shook his cudgel in the steward's face.

"It would not pain me overmuch," said he, "if here and now I belaboured thee as you deserve. But there are three reasons why that cannot be: first, I am in some haste; secondly, I never yet struck a man who could not defend himself, and thirdly, I have the colic."

Thereupon he crossed the room to where the plate-chest stood at the foot of the dais. He knew already that it contained bowls, plates and dishes of both gold and silver, and that even he and Arthur would have as much as they could do to lift it.

But, finding the right key, he opened it first, to make sure that it was full.

When Arthur-a-Bland saw the glittering mass of gold and silver, he opened his eyes wide, and wiped the back of a hairy hand across his grinning mouth.

"This night," said he, "we all feast like kings in the greenwood. We have had king's fare oft enough, but never before have we eaten off gold and silver dishes."

Not without a reason had Robin selected for this enterprise the two strongest men in his band. It was Little John who hoisted the chest upon his broad back, whilst Arthur from behind took half the weight of it upon a shoulder. And thus they went from the hall, Little John, as he passed through the doorway, handing the keys to Robin.

CHAPTER TEN

A BANQUET IN THE GREENWOOD

ROBIN HOOD, having now all the keys of the castle in his possession, and after asking pardon of the good Mistress Hamnett for the discourtesy with which he had been compelled to treat her, promptly locked the lot of them up in the great hall, and ascended the steps to the kitchen and adjoining outhouses, where he found that Little John and Arthur-a-Bland had already lifted the plate-chest into the cart, where it was hidden beneath earthenware pots, pans and ewers.

"John," said he, slapping the big man on the back, "so far our fortunes could not have prospered better, but I will never rest this night with a clear conscience till the oath I swore at Dale be well fulfilled. That rests to no small extent with thee, and you know well what to do, according to our plan. As for Arthur and I, we will to Holling Well without delay, for I chafe to get out of this potter's garb into good Lincoln green."

"Set thy mind at ease, Robin," Little John replied. "Thou shalt both dine and sleep this night better even than thy wont. I go to Bulwell now to find the Sheriff; and if I cannot lead him by the nose like a ringed hog, then my name be Small instead of Little."

Thereupon the cart began to trundle down the hill, Arthur-a-Bland, walking behind afoot, using all his strength to hold it back, in the way of a brake, since the slope was steep and the great weight of the plate-chest was too much for the jennet.

Once they were on level ground, however, the little un-groomed Spanish steed was well up to the work, and set off at an ambling trot in a northerly direction.

Little John turned sharp upon his heel and went straight back to the kitchen. There he told the cook, who was still gagged and tied to the table, that he would inconvenience him but little longer, since he was about to take his departure once and for all. He had fared well, he said, during his stay in Nottingham Castle, and he had no complaints to make. At that he crossed to the stables, where he saddled the horse he should have ridden at the hunt.

Leading the horse to the wood-shed where he had locked up the kitchen-maids, he gave the wenches a sweeping bow, doffing his feathered cap in the manner of a courtier. In his scarlet jerkin and leather riding-boots, Little John was in very truth a fine figure of a man, and there were few of the female portion of the household who had not noticed it more than once.

"Am I not a man of my word?" he asked them. "And so be Robin and all of us who serve him. But I set ye free on one condition: ye do not release our good friend, the cook, until I have had time to gain the bottom of the castle hill."

With that he swung into the saddle and set off at a canter, waving a hand at the gaunt walls of Nottingham Castle, as if he was loth to see the last of it. On the level ground he broke into a gallop, and never drew rein until he was clear of the town. Alternately walking and trotting, he at last gained Bulwell Heath, where from a hilltop he caught sight of the potter's cart in the distance. Robin and his companion were holding to a by-path that a little farther on would take them into the forest. They would be at the glade at Holling Well, Little John reckoned, in another two hours, and that would give him all the time he wanted.

Scanning the countryside in all directions, he could see no sign of the Sheriff and his huntsmen. But that mattered little, since they were bound to return to Nottingham by the main road; and there, by that time, the news would have spread from the castle to the very confines of the town that the Sheriff's plate-chest had been stolen by Robin Hood and his men.

It was a good two hours later, when Little John was riding at a walk, when he saw the hunting party coming in his direction. They were yet the better part of a mile away; but he immediately clapped spurs to his horse's flanks, and went toward them at a trot.

When he had covered about half the distance, he broke into a headlong gallop, waving his cap in the air and shouting at the top of his voice, like one who was distracted and alarmed.

The Sheriff saw him coming and recognized him at once. There was no mistaking that tall figure and brilliant scarlet suit.

"Sir Sheriff," John shouted, "I have ill news in very truth! The greatest calamity has happened that ever was!"

As he spoke, he reined in his steed so violently that he threw it back upon its haunches. The Sheriff for a moment stared at him in blank and mute amazement.

"How about thy colic," he angrily demanded. "I left thee, as I thought, a sick man, and I find thee a raving fool!"

Little John replied with the stammering voice of one in a panic, though, if there were any cause why he should find it difficult to speak, it was laughter more than fear that chuckled his words.

"There be dangers and alarms that can cure worse ills than I had," he made answer. "Master, I scarce know how to tell thee what hath happened in thy absence!"

Here he lifted a forearm to his eyes, as if he was actually about to burst into tears.

"Speak, knave!" shouted the other. "Hath the King returned from the Holy Land or what?"

"Worse than that!" moaned John. "Far worse! A thousand times far worse! Robin Hood himself hath broken into the castle and stolen your Honour's plate."

"My plate! 'Tis impossible! All that I had was locked safe in an oaken chest, and Warren had the key."

"That may be, your Honour," Little John replied. "But the chest itself be gone, and it is Robin Hood who hath got away with it."

Even now the Sheriff could not believe. He sat upon his horse, puffing, short of breath, and rolling his bulbous eyes.

"Why," he exclaimed, "it would take not less than a hundred men to break their way into the castle! And even then I have pikemen and archers enough to drive them forth quicker than they came."

"That may be, Sir Sheriff," Little John made answer. "But alas, what cannot be done by force may sometime be better done by guile! And, your Honour, I now rue the day that ever I was born, since I myself may be in part to blame. Thou knowest, sir, that man who came with the potter was my very cousin, of the name of Richard Greenleaf, whom I had not seen for many a year. How was I to tell that he had turned robber and an outlaw in the woods?"

"What meanest thou by all this talk of potters?" the Sheriff took him up. "What care I for all the potters in the kingdom, if my gold and silver plate be gone!"

"Alas, your Honour, there's the very rub of it! For, if the potter's mate were my rogue of a cousin, whom I took for an honest man, the very potter was Robin Hood himself!"

The Sheriff sat up in the saddle as if he had been pricked by a bodkin. He was now purple in the face.

"That's not the truth!" he cried.

"Even truer," said Little John, "than that my name be Reynold Greenleaf. Having entry to the castle, they took Master Warren and his men by surprise, locked them up in the hall, and were away with the plate-chest before a soul in Nottingham knew aught about it."

The Sheriff shook his fist at the sky.

"The rogue!" he cried. "The hypocritical, thrice-dyed rogue! The outrage at Dale Abbey were crime enough, but that he should so have cozened me, even in my own good keep, be more than flesh and blood can stand!"

Little John, who had drawn rein alongside the Sheriff, so that the two horses stook flank to flank, touched Master

Hamnett on an arm and spoke in an changed and more assuring voice.

"Yet take courage, sir," he said, "nothing is ever lost that can be regained. I have a notion—indeed, I am full confident—we may yet run the outlandish rogues to earth. The potter hath but a jaded jennet in his cart, and the chest be too heavy for them to journey fast. I watched them take the track that leads by Newstead and thence into the heart of Sherwood Forest. Even now they cannot be far away. Thou hast a score of men, all mounted and well armed, and may my tongue freeze in my throat and choke me, if I do not lead thee to Robin Hood!"

The Sheriff wheeled his horse, as he did so speaking over a shoulder.

"At last," he cried, "thou hast spoken sense! There be but two of them that should be culled like seeding nettles. Greenleaf, I swear to thee, if I can lodge Robin Hood in prison this very night, I will do more than forgive thee for having a footpad for a cousin. Thou shalt be made my steward, in lieu of Warren, who hath proved himself a dunderhead and fool!"

"Spoken as a true knightly sheriff!" Little John exclaimed. " 'Tis a reward that far exceeds the service. But, let us to it, master! Though we must gain on them as a hound outruns a fattened ewe, the sooner we start the chase the better."

They set forth in a body at a gallop, riding across country to the cart-track that Robin had taken into the forest. There were places where they had to slow down to a walk, because of the rabbit-holes that lay betwixt the heather and the gorse; and for this Little John thanked his stars in silence, for he was in some doubt whether Robin and Arthur-a-Bland had yet had time to gain the trysting-place in the greenwood. However, when they came upon the forest cart-track, the whole party set forward at a brisk canter, and presently found themselves beneath the shadow of the trees.

Master Hamnett—being over-bold on this occasion and also well assured that he had only two men to capture—headed the cavalcade; whereas Little John, who was ever in the forefront when there was any fighting to be done, was wise enough to drop back some way behind the others. They were not a mile from the place where Newstead Tower had been burned to the ground by Robert the Wolf and his Norman men-at-arms, when the Sheriff's horse dropped dead in its tracks with an arrow through the heart.

The men at his back reined in—and never a spear was raised nor a sword whipped from the scabbard. They could do naught but sit in their saddles, mute, motionless and gaping. So many mounted ninepins, and the king ninepin, the High Sheriff of Nottingham, was rolling head-over-heels like a wood-louse in the mire! For they were surrounded on every hand. As if they had sprung from out of the very earth, a hundred or more of Robin's men stood with bent bows under the oak trees, and they were all clad in Lincoln green.

From out of the shadows stepped Robin Hood himself, and Arthur-a-Bland was at his elbow, though they were simple potters no more. Little Much was grinning from ear to ear, and so was Stutely, Scarlock, Allen-a-Dale, Gilbert of the White Hand and all the rest of them. Even Friar Tuck was there, patting his paunch, for he knew that there would be a banquet that night such as even the greenwood seldom saw.

Robin doffed his cap as he stepped forward and bowed to the Sheriff, who had just struggled, bruised and panting, to his feet.

"Welcome to the forest, Master Sheriff!" he proclaimed. "As thy good wife did open thy hospitable door to me, so do I greet thee in my humble home."

The Sheriff could do naught but splutter in astonishment and rage.

Turning from him for a moment, Robin rapped out an order to his men, who were ranged on either side of the woodland cartway; and in a trice all the Sheriff's huntsmen were disarmed and told to hie them back to Nottingham, if they valued their lives at a groat.

Left alone in the forest, surrounded by the outlaws he had hunted in vain so long, Master Hamnett looked like a man who counted himself as good as dead already. He could not speak, and never tried to. His arms hung listless at his sides, and his face was a very picture of anguish and dismay.

Howbeit, he did not yet know Robin Hood, who stepped forward and took him not unkindly by an arm.

"Dost remember Dale Abbey?" he asked. "Hast forgotten how ungraciously thou didst refuse my invitation? And did I not then promise thee, Sir Sheriff, that I would entertain thee at a banquet worthy of your high office, under the greenwood tree?"

Even then the Sheriff could not speak. He was like a man in a daze—as, in very truth, he had some reason to be.

Unresisting, he was led a little way along a path beneath the trees, until he came to a glade where a great table was spread, and Robin's cooks were bringing forth roasted haunches of venison, steaming swansmeat, cooked hares and ducks and woodcocks. Still like a man not knowing what he does, Master Hamnett flopped down upon a bench and gazed around him at the merry company, all of whom bowed to their guest in mockery.

In the meantime, Master Hamnett, High Sheriff of Nottingham, had received the shock of his life. Not only was the banquet spread before him as rich and splendid as that which he would have eaten that very eve in the great hall of Nottingham Castle—but he was about to dine off his own gold and silver plate!

That the Sheriff had but a small appetite on that occasion meant naught to Robin Hood. He had fulfilled the oath he had made that day in Dale Abbey, when Allen was wedded to Maid Marian, and he had sworn that the Sheriff would dine with him in Sherwood Forest, whether he willed or not.

CHAPTER ELEVEN

SIR GUY OF GISBORNE

THE SHERIFF returned to Nottingham that night alone, though Robin Hood had the courtesy to accompany him as far as the margin of the forest. It was not exactly a pleasant ride, though Robin himself was in a merry mood; but Master Hamnett

sat silent in the saddle and seemed to be suffering from indiges-
tion, as if he had eaten his own gold and silver plate, instead
of the goodly fare that the dishes had contained.

When he arrived at the castle, he had short words and many
oaths for every member of his household; but it was Master
Warren, the steward, who justly or unjustly felt the full weight
of his displeasure. He had vowed vengeance against Robin
Hood before, but never with greater determination than now,
since this last exploit of the outlaw's had not only offended his
dignity, but had also touched his purse.

On thinking the matter over that night, when he lay sleepless
abed, he came to the conclusion that he could do nothing without
greater help from Sir Robert Braisse-Neuve.

In the meantime, a herald from Prince John had arrived at
Normanton Castle with the news that the Prince himself was
on the road north from Coventry with a great train of followers,
to hold a conference which would be attended by all the more
powerful rebel lords.

Many of these, such as Waldemar Fitzurse, were already
there, as well as Sir Stephen de Froy and the Templar, Sir
Geoffrey Malpert. The Wolf was never a man to let the grass
grow under his feet. Had he himself been in John's place, he
would have struck long before now, as soon as he had heard
that King Richard had been cast into a German prison. As
it was, he determined, the moment the fickle prince arrived
at Normanton, to persuade him to attack York without delay.
In that city Henry Bohun, Earl of Essex and Lord High
Constable of England, had gathered together a strong force of
nobles, knights and men-at-arms, all of whom were loyal to
the absent king. And as soon as Bohun had been brought to
heel, naught would remain but for John to march on London
against Longchamp and the Primate, Hubert Walter.

Braisse-Neuve knew that he could count on the support of
both the Bishop of Hereford and Sir Lucas Beaumanoir,
Grandmaster of the Holy Order of the Temple of Zion, who
had a following of over a hundred knightly lances. Accordingly
he sent messengers post-haste to summon these two lords to
Normanton.

The Lord Bishop took the road without delay, for he knew

that he had much to gain, if John could be safely crowned. He had with him a train of followers such as was worthy of a prince: squires, chaplains, lay brethren, and a party of mounted spearmen. Robin knew of their departure before they were a mile from Newark Castle, and lay in wait for them about midway between Nottingham and Mansfield. He had with him nearly every one of his foresters; and although they were outnumbered by those in the Bishop's cavalcade, the affair that followed can scarcely be described as a fight, since Robin and his men had it all their own way from the very start.

There were several of the Bishop's armed bodyguard who made some show of resistance; but, when a few of these had bitten the dust, the others dispersed in all directions. As for the minor churchmen and the lay brethren, they were like so many panic-stricken hens on finding a fox in the hen-run; and in less than five minutes Robin had captured not only the bishop himself, but all his sumpter mules and baggage.

"Make fast his reverend lordship to a tree!" Robin ordered. "Tie him tight as his own purse-strings!"

"Dost lay hands upon the Church?" the bishop cried.

"Aye, as readily as the Church lays hands on tithes and taxes, all of which are wrung from the poor and needy!"

"Thou art that scoundrel Robin Hood!" the Bishop indignantly exclaimed.

Robin bowed.

"I would say, at thy service, Sir Bishop, were it not that thou art now at mine. I have to overhaul your lordship's money-bags before I set thee free."

"Such money as I have with me," the Bishop answered, "is not mine, but the property of Mother Church."

"It will soon be that of Father Robin, every groat thou hast."

It was the sorriest day in the Bishop's life, for he loved money more than aught else, and cared not how he came by it. As for Robin, as he said himself, it was the fattest goose that he had ever plucked. Nor would he be the only one to gain by it, since there was many a Saxon serf and widowed wife in Sherwood Forest who had had to beg their bread from door to door, because of the Church's greed and the taxes levied to pay for the Holy wars.

"Not one of these poor folk, Sir Bishop," he declared, "but shall now thank thee for thy most generous bounty. If I rob Peter, it is but to pay Paul—which, when Peter be overfed and Paul be starved, seemeth to me not so much robbery as justice."

"Justice!" growled his lordship. "Who art thou to talk of justice? The hangman's noose is all the justice that in due time will come thy way, if thou dost not die unshriven in the greenwood."

"Then," quoth Robin, "if I be so great a sinner, and my merry men are sharers in my sins, it is well for us that we have a Bishop handy, to save us for a better world. Thou shalt sing us a Mass. Last time we met, I robbed thee of a wedding; and to make amends for that, thou shalt now hold a service in the greenwood."

Apart from the plight in which he found himself, the Bishop could scarce refuse to fulfil his holy office. He was unbound by Robin's orders; and with Robin Hood's foresters all bareheaded and clad in Lincoln green, kneeling around him on their sward, he then and there held Mass in Sherwood Forest.

Throughout the brief service he had no just reason to complain of either irreverence or inattention on the part of his outlawed congregation. With lowered heads, they murmured the responses; and when the Bishop had pronounced his benediction, Robin thanked him and told him he would see him safely through the forest on the road to Derby, since there were common footpads and cutpurses on the roads who were never friends of his.

It was with Will Scarlock and David of Doncaster that Robin set out that evening to escort the bishop to the outskirts of Derby town. All three of them carried their long-bows slung across their shoulders and swords at their belts. They were but two miles from Derby, and passing in single file along a woodland path where it was so dark that they could see naught but the white mule the Bishop rode, when upon a sudden they heard the thrum of a bowstring and an arrow whistled through the thickets, to bury itself deep in David's shoulder.

The Doncaster man fell forward upon the neck of his horse, letting out a groan that was scarce audible; and on the instant

Robin bent his bow and shot from the saddle. He had seen no more than a vague shadow in the undergrowth, but that was enough for him. To snatch the bow from his shoulder and fix a shaft to the string was the work of a moment—and all they heard was a thud and a groan, whilst a man pitched forward on his face, to lie huddled and motionless upon the pathway.

Even before that, another man had seized the bridle of the Bishop's mule; and, no sooner had he done so than he dropped like a log under a stroke from Will Scarlock's sword. Howbeit, there was yet a third rascal there, who dived across the pathway, as if all he meant to do was to make good his escape whilst there was time. But Robin was too quick for him. Swinging down from the saddle, and knowing that he had not time to draw, he let out with a fist and sent the man rolling upon the dead leaves beneath the trees.

It was at that moment, as it happened, that the moon came out from behind a cloud and fell upon the features of Robin's victim, who was now pinned to the ground with the Saxon outlaw on his chest.

Robin peered into his face, and then broke into a laugh.

"I killed never a man in cold blood yet," said he, "but, if it were within me so to do, by Saint Dunstan, I would do it now!"

The Bishop had tumbled from his mule, but he stood upright on his feet, and—again to do him justice—he once more proved that he was a man of mettle, though he had taken no active part in the fight.

"What's this?" he cried. "If these be common cutpurses, ye have made the shortest work of them that ever I did see!"

"He that I have here be worse than any footpad that ever laid in wait on Watling Street," Robin made reply. " 'Tis the very man of whom I warned your Holiness: a knight of the night, who makes of murder his one and only trade. Sir Guy of Gisborne. I have sought him with an arrow often enough, but never did I think to have the scoundrel under my knee."

The man who answered, who lay flat upon his back, spoke in a voice that was both harsh and husky.

"Robin Hood," said he, "it be my misfortune that we do not meet on better terms. To speak the truth, I took ye, in the darkness, to be three lay brethren travelling with a fat abbot, and I find myself over-matched by the rogue who claims all Sherwood as his own."

"And so it be," said Robin. "I have made it my business to clean up the greenwood of human wolves as well as the King's deer. I could slay thee now—and I swear I would think naught of it—had I thy custom of committing murder on the high road. Howbeit, Sir Guy, I am moulded in another fashion. I give thee fair play such as you never gave to any man. Get thee to thy feet, draw thy sword, and defend thyself as best ye may."

That was a rare duel in the pale moonlight under the greenwood trees. Two men lay dead upon the pathway. David of Doncaster, with the blood streaming from his wounded shoulder, had seated himself upon a fallen tree-trunk. Will Scarlock and the Bishop stood aside and never uttered a word after the sharp swords had rung together.

Sir Guy, pressing the attack from the very start, drove Robin back, until he stumbled on a tree-root and came within an ace of losing his life. He saved himself only by stepping aside in the very nick of time, so that his opponent's sword-thrust passed him. Shifting his ground, Robin now took and held the advantage, until he had forced his adversary against the trunk of an oak tree.

The robber knight of Gisborne then recognised himself for lost, else he would never have practised a foul stroke. Grasping the blade of Robin's sword in his left hand, he drew back his sword to put a quick end to the business. But again Robin was too quick for him. Though his sword was held, he had his left hand free; and with this, before Sir Guy could strike, he caught him a blow with his fist. A knockout on the chin dropped the Gisborne outlaw like a stone; and even before he had touched the ground, Robin had wrenched his sword free and pierced him through the heart.

"A foul end to a foul life!" said he. "What think you, Sir Bishop? There lies a man more fit for the gallows than I."

The Bishop could not but agree. That night he had seen a different Robin Hood than the man who had defied him in Dale Abbey. Nonetheless, he could not forget that he had been robbed of much of his wordly goods—and that, as it were, stuck in his throat, making it difficult for him to breathe.

Robin turned to David of Doncaster and soon satisfied himself that his wound was not serious, though the flow of blood had been great. Leaving David in charge of Scarlock, Robin went on ahead with the Bishop, and before long came to a hilltop on the Belper Road whence they could look down upon the lights of Derby.

"And now holiness and roguery must part," said he. "Go thy ways, my lord, to Normanton, and there do thy worst. But never think that I know naught of the traitor's plot that will be hatched. And if it is not beneath thy reverend dignity to give a message from Robin Hood to my lord, the Baron of Normanton and Hautbray, whom men rightly call the Wolf, tell him this from me: I am king in the greenwood as Richard is King of England, and he will not find it easy to rob either of his crown."

CHAPTER TWELVE

NORMANTON CASTLE

THE GREAT castle at Normanton, that Robert Braisse-Neuve had built upon a hill, was all in preparation for the arrival of Prince John. A few of the superior knights and nobles, such as the Grandmaster of the Templars, were housed within the castle walls; but most were encamped without with their squires and men-at-arms, making in all a great number of both horse and foot, each lord and knight with his banner planted and unfurled before his tent.

Such was the ennobling sight that good Master Hamnett, the Sheriff of Nottingham, beheld, when he rode up the hill, attended by a party of his own officers and archers. Derby town itself, and especially the low-lying market-place upon the river bank, had been crowded for days with Norman soldiery and sutlers, and the keepers of the wine-shops and taverns had been doing a roaring trade.

The Sheriff, without the retinue that had come with him, was immediately admitted across the draw-bridge, and thence was conducted to a room where he found the baron in conference with Beaumanoir, Fitzurse, the Bishop of Hereford and Sir Stephen de Froy—who were the chief leaders of the insurrection. But it was the Wolf himself who was the brains of the rebellion, as well as the very hammer-head, as it were, of the blow with which he meant to smite the crown from off the head of the imprisoned King. He had already worked out, in his own cunning, crafty way, every detail of the plan he now urged upon his fellow conspirators. Nearly all the midlands, due mainly to his own energy and efforts, were on the side of the Prince; for those who, like the thane of Sherwood, had refused to muster under the banner that displayed a red wolf's head upon a field of gold, had met with the same unhappy fate, and Newstead Tower was not the only Saxon castle between Leicester and Ashby-de-la-Zouche that had been left in smouldering ruins.

And now that he considered the iron was hot for the striking, Braisse-Neuve counselled attacking and subduing Bohun's men at York before Prince John marched south at the head of his army to London.

"A dagger stroke," he argued, "swift, sudden, and delivered with a short arm, for York city lieth not over far from here. It is the Earl of Essex and his men who must first be vanquished, for we would be ill-advised to move southward with his army in our rear. Besides, as High Constable of England, he wields an influence that makes delay a double danger; for, from all reports that have come to me, what he calls his loyalty to Cœur-de-lion spreads already like the plague, and the longer we leave him unmolested, the more men will he have under his standard. Leave rats alone, my lords, and they will breed; and hence I urge most strongly that we persuade the Prince to strike hence at York as soon as he hath joined us."

"Good words and better sense, my lord!" Beaumanoir exclaimed. "That was never Richard's way in the Holy Land, for he would ever attack the Turk at his very strongest point, and more than once he paid for it more dearly than he liked."

It was at this juncture that the Sheriff of Nottingham was

ushered into the room; and he was seen to be nervous and to falter somewhat, before he bowed to the company, each in turn. For Master Hamnett may have been a great man in Nottingham, but he was immediately and painfully made conscious that he was but small fry in the presence of these high and mighty lords. Nor was he put much more at his ease by Braisse-Neuve's curt and sneering welcome.

"Ho, ho!" he exclaimed. "Hast come to Normanton, Master Sheriff, to find a safe asylum from the outlaw of Sherwood Forest? Methinks, this be a case of the cockerel hunting the fox. I hear now that he hath gutted Nottingham Castle itself, and my Lord Bishop here be skinned as cleanly as the self-same rogue ever skinned a hart."

"It is upon that very business, my Lord Baron," the Sheriff made reply, swallowing his indignation and his pride, "that I am come hither this day, though it be news to me that your lordship knoweth already the outrage I have suffered."

"Aye," the Wolf chuckled, "I have long ears, forsooth, like all of my breed; and I would have thee remember, too, that ill tidings ever travel swift upon the wings of mockery. In other words, good master, thou art a fool, and this Robin Hood hath made thee look an even greater one."

The Sheriff could do naught but shrug his shoulders and throw out both his hands.

"Other fish have been caught in the same net," he surlily replied. "Ask my Lord Bishop here. Though he was attended by a bodyguard, the villain robbed him of all he had."

"Bah!" the baron cried, striking the table with a fist. "Had you been better fitted for thine office, he would have been brought to the gallows long before now. There is no greater knave in all England; yet there is none freer than he to work his will as he may."

"The scoundrel hath certain redeeming features," the Bishop interposed, with his eyes downcast as if speaking to himself. "Robber and outlaw he may be, but he hath a sense of fairness, and I am not like to forget that he saved my life."

The Wolf burst into a roar of laughter—and his mirth was no pleasant thing to see.

"He scattered thy men and lay brethren like a flock of rooks, crammed his pockets from the coffers of the Church, and then saved thy life! I think even now, my Lord Bishop, he owes ye much, and more than he is ever like to pay. But what is thy business, Master Hamnett? Know that we have weightier matters to attend to than the hanging of a hedge-thief."

"Before he may be hanged, he must first be caught," the Sheriff answered, being encouraged to speak more boldly, since the Bishop of Hereford seemed ready to support any request that he might make. "I do assure thee, my lord, if we had but five thousand men-at-arms to beat Sherwood!"

His speech was cut short by another thump on the table that made even the Bishop start.

"By the holy rood!" Braisse-Neuve shouted. "Five thousand men! Am I deaf or a fool or both? When we must march on York with every lance, spear and crossbow we can muster, when we must match our strength against that of a tried soldier like Henry Bohun, am I to give thee five thousand men-at-arms to round up a common cutpurse!"

There followed a brief silence, during which the Sheriff again shrugged his shoulders, as if he gave the matter up as hopeless. Then it was de Froy who spoke, and it was the first time he had opened his mouth since the Sheriff had been shown into the room.

"In my thinking," said he, "there be sense in what appears like folly, as is often enough the case."

"Dost support a lawyer's strategy and call thyself a knight!" cried the baron, scowling at Sir Stephen. "Ha, but I had forgotten Dale Abbey! Thou wouldst readily forsake our cause to hang the man who robbed thee of a bride."

De Froy sprang to his feet.

"My lord," he answered, "I am not one to brook such words from any man! That were enough to warrant my gauntlet in thy face!"

The Wolf had also risen, and would, it maybe, have accepted a challenge that was never given, had not the Grandmaster intervened.

"Enough!" he cried. "Hot blood means words that cannot be recalled. Sir Stephen and my lord of Normanton, where goeth chivalry, I ask of you, if two such gallant knights would quarrel about a thief? And what hope have we that our cause can prosper, if some of us are so eager to fight among ourselves? Sir Stephen must have had a reason for what he said—of that I am sure. I ask thee, my lord, to hear him out, and then, I feel certain, thou wilt withdraw the words thou used."

The Wolf, as was his custom, chuckled softly to himself. If he was aware that he had made a serious mistake, for that he blamed the Sheriff who had considerably annoyed him. However, he had his own way of getting out of difficulties.

"Think no more of it!" he declared. "Remember, Sir Stephen, that day in Dale Abbey, I was made to look an even greater fool than thou, and that may be why I taunted thee. Forget it, I beseech thee, and thou shouldst find that all the easier when I admit that I could never hope to stand in open fight against so bold and proved a champion. Come, therefore, let us get back to our muttons: you cannot think that this same Robin Hood is more dangerous to our cause than the Earl of Essex, the High Constable of England!"

De Froy had also calmed down, though he knew well enough in his heart that it was because of Marian that he wished to bring the outlaw to the hangman's noose.

"I speak as a friend and as a soldier," he made answer. "Though I hold no brief for Richard, he would never attack in the Holy wars or elsewhere without seeing to it that both flanks were covered. Now, my lords, I pray your attention for a moment. It is generally agreed, I take it, that we strike hence at York; may I point out that we cannot do so without having on our right flank the northern confines of Sherwood Forest."

"I take thy meaning," Braisse-Neuve answered. "But what hath an army such as ours to fear from some two hundred archers?"

Sir Stephen shook his head in doubt.

"The villain can muster more men than that," he went on, "and many of them, as we know to our cost, the finest bowmen in the country."

Braisse-Neuve was silent a moment, thinking. He had an idea already that Sir Stephen was in the right, but, being obstinate by nature, he still stuck to his point.

"Mailed men-at-arms and armoured knights against Saxon

yeomen!" he protested, throwing out a hand. "It seemeth to me that we should make short work of them, if they should venture to attack."

"That will they never do," de Froy answered. "We must pass through wooded country, for I know the Yorkshire dales; and they will keep to the woods, and never a sight of them will we get. As for pursuit, that would be folly, for the very reason you have mentioned, my lord: chain-mail suits its purpose, but no man who wears it can ever be fleet of foot. Take my word for it, therefore, they will harry our flank all the road from Stavely to the north of Doncaster."

This silenced Braisse-Neuve, whereas from the others there came a murmur of applause. There was no question but that Sir Stephen knew his business as a soldier.

It was Sir Lucas Beaumanoir, the Grandmaster, who asked the next question.

"Then what dost thou suggest?"

"With the Prince coming hither," de Froy replied, "we cannot detach so strong a force as five thousand, as my good Master Sheriff has proposed. But I am willing—with your sanction, my lords—to march at the head of five hundred into the very heart of the forest between Nottingham and Mansfield. Such a manœuvre may serve a double purpose: I may be able to force the outlaw and his men to open combat, and thus bring him to book; and in any case I will hold him south of Barnesdale, so that the road be clear for the Prince to march on York."

Not one of them, not even the Wolf himself, could dispute the wisdom of such tactics. And thus it was that, after all, the Sheriff had his way. And two days after, Sir Stephen de Froy set forth upon the road by Ilkeston to Newark. This took him, as he had said himself it would, into the very heart of Sherwood Forest. And what befell him there deserves a place in another chapter.

CHAPTER THIRTEEN

THE DEVIL UNCHAINED

WHEN HE marched into Sherwood Forest, Sir Stephen had with him, as well as that other knight, the vain Templar, Sir Geoffrey Malpert, a mixed force of five hundred Norman spearmen and archers, armed with cross-bows. All went afoot, except the knights themselves and their esquires, for he knew well enough that horses would be more hindrance than help upon the narrow woodland paths, where even one who walks must often stoop to avoid the branches of the trees.

All the same, the knight, being well advised as to the nature of the country, intended to try and draw Robin and his men out of the woods, thinking that all the advantage would be on his side, could he but meet the outlaws in the open. With this intent he proceeded to the high moorlands north of Newstead that even to this day are known as the Robin Hood Hills, and there pitched his camp.

Becoming impatient, and hearing the news that Prince John had already arrived at Normanton, de Froy sent scouting parties into the Forest and this was the first serious mistake he made; for a goodly number of those men never came back to him, and those who did had a sorry tale to tell.

They had been waylaid and captured in the forest, and then deprived of their armour, their money and their weapons. Moreover, they all had the same report to make—a report that somewhat shook Sir Stephen's confidence: though days had passed and de Froy's sentries had never seen a sign of an enemy, the woods on every hand were said to be swarming with green-clad bowmen, whose numbers seemed to be increasing every day.

Sir Stephen, sitting sulking in his tent like another Achilles, held council with Sir Geoffrey—who was no more use to his commander than his over-weighted battleaxe was to him. It seemed to de Froy that but three courses lay open to him, not one of which was much to his liking: he might remain where he was, and stay there till doomsday, or he might march through the forest to Nottingham or Derby. The latter, of course, would be an admission that his enterprise had failed, and he had no mind to face either the sneers of Robert Braisse-Neuve or the fury of Prince John. He had no idea that the Prince had already left Normanton Castle in greater haste than he had come, in circumstances and for a reason that we shall presently proceed to explain. For the nonce, we are concerned with the gallant knight, Sir Stephen de Froy, and of his valour there was never a question. His strategy had been sound enough, but he had fallen into the error of imagining that his adversary would do exactly what he wanted him to do—and that had never been Robin's way.

For Robin had seen him coming long before the knight had pitched his camp. At the western end of those hills that are clad in gorse and heather and which look down upon the forest, there is a rocky eminence in which there is a niche like a huge arm-chair. It was from this point of vantage that he had seen the Norman force approaching, and at once he had dispatched his messengers west to Alfreton and north to Barnesdale. Little John sounded his horn in the vale of the Don by Swinton; Will Stutely summoned Robin's men in the woods around Southwell, whereas Scarlock blew three blasts in Darley Dale, and within three hours had fifty archers at his back. From north, east and west they hastened to Newstead at the bidding of the outlawed king of the greenwood—with the result that the next day de Froy's five hundred men-at-arms were surrounded by three hundred outlaws, whose Lincoln green jerkins and hose were invisible among the undergrowth.

And even then Robin would not attack. In spite of the fact that numbers were against him, he had little doubt that he could defeat the Normans in an open fight, but he knew that he could not do so without losing many lives. And Robin's merry men were more to him that the lives of Norman rebels and all the plunder he would find in Sir Stephen's camp.

As for that knight, allowing a week to pass, and finding that the mice he wanted were not disposed to walk into what he had thought might prove a trap, he gave orders to strike camp, and taking the shortest route to Nottingham, marched into the forest.

That was his undoing, and all that Robin had been waiting for. Of the fight that followed, there is nothing much to be said, since one combat is very like another. The Normans, even the cross-bowmen, were at a disadvantage in the woods. De Froy himself behaved throughout with the valour for which he was noted, and would have been slain a score of times, had it not been that he was wearing a suit of the finest Spanish armour that he had often worn in Gascony. By the strange irony of fate, the combat took place within a few furlongs of the ruins of Newstead Tower the Saxon castle where Robin should have ruled as franklin and where his father had been foully slain by Robert Braisse-Neuve. Rallying his scattered soldiers and rescuing more than half his baggage, de Froy fought his way to the castle, which—it will be remembered—was surrounded by a wooden palisade. Gaining these ancient entrenchments and the demolished castle walls, he turned like a tiger at bay, fully confident that he and his men could there hold their own.

All the same, he was forced from the very start to realise that he would have to undergo a siege, for once again he was encompassed, and within a far smaller circumference than before. An assault he feared less than that starvation in the end might compel him to surrender; and rather than do that he swore an oath that he would plunge his sword into himself before he delivered it into the hands of the man who had robbed him of his bride. And there we must leave him, for the nonce, and even Robin Hood himself; for, whilst these things were happening, an event of historical importance had taken place in England.

It was an event that set all the country by the ears, from the Tweed to the Isle of Wight, that came as a boon to many and as a shock to others—and of the latter, none felt it more than that traitor prince, John of Anjou, whom we left upon the road to Normanton from Ashby-de-la-Zouche.

When he and his cavalcade marched through the old Danish town of Derby, he looked upon himself as already King of England; and in very truth he had brought with him a vast and regal retinue. At Ashby, the Prince, when a self-invited guest at the castle there, had helped himself to whatsoever he wanted, since the lord of the place, the Earl of Winchester, was absent in the Holy Land; and over and above that, he had plundered the surrounding country in so ruthless a manner that he stirred up bitter hatred against himself before ever he came to the throne.

With Sir Robert Braisse-Neuve, however, he knew that he could take no such liberties; and he certainly had no reason to complain of the right royal welcome the baron gave him so soon as ever he had passed under the portcullis at Normanton. And that very day they held a council in one of the upper chambers that was attended by all the more powerful lords who had attached themselves to John. These included, of course, those whom we have seen before: Waldemar Fitzurse, the Bishop of Hereford and the Grandmaster, who, with the Wolf himself, soon succeeded in persuading the fickle prince that they must strike first at York before marching south on London.

It may be truly said that John had no single virtue nor redeeming feature in a character that was more evil than that of any other monarch who ever sat upon the throne of England—with the sole exception that he was very far from a fool. Treacherous, he may have been, passionate, deceitful, cowardly and pitiless, but he had a kind of quick sly instinct that was seldom at fault; and he readily fell in with Braisse-Neuve's plan.

At that time there were only two men in England whom he had any cause to fear: one of these was Hubert Walter, the new Primate, and the other was Henry Bohun, Earl of Essex and Lord High Constable. There was yet another whom he feared more than these two put together, whom he spoke of as the Devil, and that was his warrior brother whom he believed to be secure behind prison bars.

As a matter of fact, it was John himself who might be likened to the Devil, whereas Richard had many of the qualities that, in those days, the lion was supposed to possess. However, since of two evils it is ever better to choose the least, the vast majority of the people of England, whether Anglo-Saxon or Norman, preferred the warrior-king to the fickle, luxury-loving prince, and there were few of them who did not wish to see Richard home again. As for luxury, John had his fill of it that evening, when he dined in the great hall at Derby with the Baron of Normanton and Hautbray as his host. Never had the Wolf himself, who cared not what he ate, dined so regally, for the Prince had brought his own cooks, as well as both rich wines and various delicacies from foreign parts.

John himself drank deeply, as was his custom; and before the feast was ended he was flushed with overfeeding and the way in which he had mixed old wine and new ale. Indeed, raising a silver beaker, he drank to the future King of England; and even as the vain toast was cheered to the echo in the hall, a rider came spurring up the hill. And it was this messenger who brought the pregnant news that we have mentioned before.

He had left London early the previous day. He had changed horses at Bedford, Northampton and Market Harborough; and the steed he rode was so spent when he climbed the castle hill at Derby that he had to dismount and drag it by the reins. Nor was he himself in much better plight, for he had halted only for meals and was smothered from head to spur in dust and foam from the horse's mouth. Nonetheless, declaring that the news he brought was urgent, he insisted upon being taken at once into the presence of the Prince, even though His Highness was still seated at the banquet.

John scowled when he saw him, thinking it an affront to his princely dignity that so disreputable a knave should have been admitted; but his face changed in a trice when he saw the seal at the foot of the billet that he had snatched impatiently from the man's hand. He had read the words—which were but nine in number—three or four times, before the scroll fell from his hand to the floor.

Braisse-Neuve stooped down, picked up the billet from the floor, and read as follows:

"Take heed to thyself, since the Devil be unchained."

John had fallen back in his chair, like one in a daze, with his eyes staring blankly at the table. The Wolf rose swiftly to his feet, drew the messenger aside, and plied him with quick and whispered questions.

Then he returned to the Prince, who had risen to his feet

as if he were drunk—as indeed he was, for he was now drunk with fear as well as wine.

"It is the worst, as you said!" he rapped out. "Richard hath not only escaped, he is even now in London. And that means we must strike, and strike at once. If we can cook Bohun's goose, we shall have all the north behind us."

John was now trembling like a man with ague.

"Fool!" he cried. "Fool! Would thou pit thyself against my brother? Art so vain and blind that thou cannot read the writing on the wall? I tell thee, all is lost! Those of us who are wise had best fly the country."

Braisse-Neuve scowled in anger. A dark flush spread across his lean and shrivelled countenance, and for a moment it looked as if he was about to strike the prince whom he had sworn to serve.

"I croak no such raven's song!" he growled between clenched teeth. "If thou my lord, will not fight for the crown thou covet, then I at least shall maintain my baronage and knighthood, or die like a dog in a ditch!"

"You rave!" said John, who by now had found his voice. "And raving mad thou must be! Because thou hast a strong keep here, dost think that thou art stronger and can defy the Devil? I know better, as I know my brother better. He will take thy castle, were it walls of iron, and then thou wouldst, in truth, die in a ditch, as thou sayest!"

With these words, the Prince clutched his head with both hands—even tugged his hair, as if he would pluck it forth by the roots. And in such great and dishonourable distress, he stumbled forth from the room. And an hour later, accompanied by only a small party of knights and their attendants, he was riding west to Chester.

CHAPTER FOURTEEN

THE BLACK KNIGHT

AS THE SUN set over London town, on the very evening when Prince John fled from Derby, two men stood upon the roof of the White Tower and looked down upon the river.

They were very different men, both in personal appearance and the manner of their attire. The one was a little under the middle height, narrow of shoulder, yet upright in his bearing. Indeed, the hooked nose, thin lips and clear-cut features, together with the resolution that was patent in these features, gave him the aspect of a soldier, which his garb belied. For he wore a long clerical mantle of the very finest Flanders cloth, of which both the collar and the sleeves were adorned with fur, whilst upon his chest a golden cross, hanging from his neck on a golden chain, caught the red light of the setting sun. He was clean-shaven, and about his lips there played a generous smile—the smile of one who has accomplished something of which he has every reason to be proud.

His companion stood above him by more than head and shoulders, and was proportionately broad and deep of chest. He was bearded and blue of eye, his face tanned by semi-tropic suns. Beneath the long silken Norman robe one could see, when he moved, the rigidity of a suit of armour. Indeed, a brace of steel chain gauntlets lay upon the parapet before him; and the two hands, upon which he rested his huge weight on the sill of an embrasure, looked as if they could strangle a man in their grip as though he were but a hen.

Only a few minutes before, in the great council chamber under their feet, these two had been seated at the head of a long oaken table, around which sat every important baron, noble and lord, both spiritual and temporal, in the south of England; and this in itself should be enough to suggest to the reader that the first of these two was Hubert Walter, Archbishop of Canterbury, and the other, Cœur-de-lion, King Richard the First of England.

When the Great Council had dispersed, they had ascended the narrow spiral steps to the leads of the White Tower that they might at once breathe fresher air and look down upon the London that had so joyfully that day greeted the return of the pilgrim warrior-king. Richard's eyes, as he leaned upon the parapet, were gazing downward at a square tower upon the river bank beneath which there was a broad low archway that conducted the river water into the moat. He knew the history of that tower—for even in those days it had a history, though it was destined to behold many a tragedy thereafter. It had originally been built by William Rufus, but the river had eaten into the foundations and the outer walls had crumbled. Henry the Second, Richard's father, had rebuilt it, by way of a penance for the murder of Thomas-à-Becket. It was this at which King Richard now pointed with a finger.

"Thither," said he, "were I a different man than I be, would I send my brother."

The Primate's smile broadened, as he shook his head.

"Not thy mother's son, sire. Any other man, I will allow; and I would not give a groat for his life."

"You are right," said the King. "There is more than one of them who will pay dear for this treachery; nor will I be over-cautious whom I spare. But I have yet to get tidings from the north. Bohun may have dispersed the traitors before I get there, though I start at daybreak to-morrow."

"There is little news yet come to hand," said Walter. "The Prince was last heard of at Ashby. They evidently intended to move on York, for they threw out a party under Stephen de Froy to guard their flank that touched on Sherwood Forest. And there—believe it or not, sire, as you will—they were caught by that scoundrel Robin Hood and are now besieged in the ruins of Newstead Tower."

Richard turned quickly, and laid one of his great hairy hands upon the Primate's shoulder.

"Tell me more of this knave?" he asked. "If half I have heard of him be true, he seems a greater rival for my crown than my poor shiftless brother!"

Hubert Walter laughted.

"That would be no more than fact," said he, "if all thy kingdom were but Sherwood Forest. However, there is this to be said for him: he is an outlaw more by misfortune than by choice. It was this Robin's father, Alfred, Thane of Sherwood, who refused to march with his men under Braisse-Neuve's banner——"

"Aye, I know the story," Richard shouted, in a voice that had something in it of the angry roar of a lion. "And so soon as ever I can lay hands on him, the old Wolf goes to a quicker death than ever he gave the Saxon franklin! I know Braisse-Neuve of old; and though he has fought for Christendom, even in Palestine, he was more Saladin's friend than mine. A wolf he hath ever been, but, I swear by the splendour of Our Lady's brow, he shall now feel the teeth of a lion!"

For a while after that, they talked of many things, of the most pressing affairs of state, before Richard laid his head upon his pillow. And even then he must have slept but little that night, for he was seen to enter the Chapel of St. John in the small hours of the morning, and there go down upon his knees, thanking God, it may be, that his kingdom had been restored to him.

Nonetheless, he was up betimes, at daybreak on the morrow, to leave London by Cripple Gate, and riding north on Watling Street, attended by two hundred knights whose worth and valour he had learned to trust in Palestine.

They journeyed by easy stages; and in consequence three days were passed before they were north of Leicester; for, before they had crossed the Bedford Ouse, they were met by a courier from the Lord High Constable, the Earl of Essex, with the news that John had fled, his soldiery had scattered, and Sir Robert Braisse-Neuve had shut himself up in Normanton Castle.

Richard could have asked for nothing better, for the victory was already his without a blow being struck. Bohun was marching southward through Sheffield, and all the north had declared openly for the King.

It was in Charnwood Forest that Richard, having heard upon the road further tales of Robin Hood, ordered his knights to go on ahead without him. As for himself, he had some private business to attend to. He had exchanged his shield, the royal escutcheon that bore the lion's head, for one without coat-of-arms or any sort of design; and he was dressed in a suit of black steel armour upon which there was nothing to disclose his rank.

More than one of the lords who accompanied him protested that it was folly, at such a time, for him to expose himself alone. For all that, there was not one of them who did not know that such protestations were altogether useless; for Richard was now about to embark upon such an adventure as he loved. It was past midday when he set forth upon the road which passes between Nottingham and Derby, and shortly before sunset he entered Sherwood Forest to the south of Heanor.

Now it so happened that, upon that very evening, Little John, with whom were Will Scarlock, Arthur-a-Bland and Friar Tuck, had gone into Ilkeston to fetch a vat of Chian wine that had there been hidden for many months. The four outlaws had taken a cart into Ilkeston, between the shafts of which was that very Spanish jennet that had carried the potter's wares to Nottingham and which now pulled the vat of Chian wine. They were under the western extremity of the Robin Hood Hills when Little John, who was mounted on a horse, bethought him of riding up to Robin's Seat, to see if he could discover aught of interest in the surrounding country. A glimpse of a wild boar or a grazing herd of deer was the most that he expected, when to his astonishment he beheld upon a pathway that ran in a north-easterly direction a Norman knight-at-arms.

"What Heaven-sent fool be this!" he muttered to himself. "Is it one of the wolf-pack from Normanton or some madcap errant knight who thinks he can raise the siege of Newstead with a single sword?"

Keeping under cover of the heather, he crawled back to his steed, which he had left near the bottom of the hill, and in less than ten minutes he had rejoined his comrades.

"Here cometh a goose for the plucking," he informed them, "and a black goose, by the look of him, which be always the better eating! Come, run the cart from the road under the trees, where that four-legged friend of ours will graze as quiet as any sheep! This armoured idiot cometh this way on the same road, and it should be easy to take him as to shake an over-ripe apple from a tree."

The thing was no sooner said than done. Scarlock and the friar took both the cart and John's horse from the roadway to a place where they were well hidden by intervening undergrowth and where there was grass for them to graze. Arthur and Little John, in the meantime, had taken post behind a hedge of blackthorn, where they were soon joined by Friar Tuck and Will. The friar was unarmed, save for a great cudgel that he had taken out of the cart, but the other three carried both long-bows and swords.

As these three fitted arrows to their bow-strings, the friar could not resist the temptation of helping himself to some of the blackberries that were ripe for plucking; nor could he refrain, a moment later, from a great smacking of his lips.

"Hist!" Little John cautioned him. "How can we hear the hoofs of a horse approaching when the Church must refresh itself at the wayside?"

The friar took no notice, but went on eating, carefully selecting such berries as were blackest, biggest and most juicy.

As for the knight, he was not then two hundred yards away from them. He was sitting well back in the saddle, with the reins loose, and actually humming a tune, which sounded somewhat like the noise within a seashell, since his vizor was closed. With his sword sheathed and his great lance at rest, he apparently had no knowledge that there were four outlaws lying in wait for him; nor, for that matter, did he seem to care.

As soon as he came within sight, it was Arthur-a-Bland, who whispered in the friar's ear.

"By Saint Dunstan!" he exclaimed. "Be this Gog and Magog rolled into one! Never saw I such a man before better worthy of cudgelling, and methinks I would have my work cut out to baste him, even without his armour."

The friar took no notice, but went ahead with his blackberries, though a moment later he drew the stave from his hempen belt; and when the black knight had drawn level with them,

all four sprang upon a sudden to their feet, and it was Little
John who gave the challenge.

"Hold, Sir Knight!" he cried. "We are marksmen good
enough to find a joint in thy harness. Attempt to draw thy
sword, and we let fly with our shafts!"

The knight reined in his horse and turned in the saddle,
resting a hand upon the animal's haunches. He seemed in no
way alarmed; and his voice, when he spoke, was both slow
and deep in tone.

"I call this right honest courtesy," he remarked; "ye would
slay me for drawing the sword I bear in honour, and ye
bring a priest to shrive me before I die! By that, good sirs, I
see ye can be no common footpads, but honest English yeomen
with a sense of true religion."

At those words the three cloth-yard shafts that had been
directed straight at the knight were slowly lowered; and it
was Will Scarlock who spoke.

"True words enough," said he, "though they may be spoken
in jest! Strange though it may seem to you, Sir Knight, we
claim the right to question any man who passes on these roads."

The knight paused before he answered, though he never
moved an inch, but still reclined upon the saddle.

"And from whom hold ye this right?" he asked.

"From one Robin Hood," Scarlock answered. "Of whom
ye may have heard."

"That is true. I have heard some mention of his name from
time to time, if I remember aright. But I was in error, it
seems, in thinking this forest was the King's domain."

The friar, with his mouth and chin all stained with berry
juice, stepped boldly into the roadway.

"*Dei gratia*," he observed, "these woods belong to the King;
but, *de facto*, *deo volente*, they are the realm of Robin Hood.
Explained otherwise, Sir Knight, my meaning runneth thus:
God gave this forest to His Majesty, and all living things that
are found herein he did likewise present to Robin Hood."

The black knight threw back his helmeted head, roared
with laughter, and swung down from the saddle.

"It delights me much," he said, "to meet with a priest so
scholarly! Methought, by the look of you, good brother,

thou wert more fond of blackberries than of Latin. As for thy fellows, I so like the look of them that I would fain meet your master. Come, take me to him! You will find me as easy to lead as any lamb on a leash."

Nothing in the world could have looked less like a lamb, as he took a few strides forward, his black armour clanking with the movement of his heavy and gigantic limbs.

"Stay!" cried Little John, though he had hitched his bow upon a shoulder. "It be no such easy matter as that, to be admitted to the court of King Robin. We would know first, Sir Knight, whence thou comest and wither thou wouldst go?"

"I am journeying to York, and being a stranger to these parts, I have missed the road."

"Aye, indeed, thou hast! Thou goest in the wrong direction —and yet also on the right; for those in York be loyal to Cœur-de-lion, the same as we be, though we pay ourselves for our loyalty by eating royal venison and relieving the Church, so far as we may, of the temptation that ensues from riches."

The black knight laughed again, and, extending a hand, laid it upon Little John's shoulder.

"Thou art a man after mine own heart," said he, "though I will give way to thee in nothing, save the trifling matter of an inch or so in height. By the holy rood, though I have spoken to thee and thy friends no more than five minutes, I have learned more of England in that time than I ever knew before!"

"Then we will show thee even more," Little John made answer. "We have a pack of Norman rebels shut up, like foxes run to earth, in the ruins of Newstead Tower, where Robin of Sherwood should be thane. We be loyal men, though law-breakers; and if you swear to us that you are loyal to the King, we will take you even now to Robin Hood."

The black knight lifted his great fist and shook it at the sky.

"If I be not loyal to King Richard," he declared, "then he is false to himself; and you have that from me by the many oaths I know!"

That was enough for Little John and his comrades. There and then they got the cart out from the underwoods, and the five of them set forth upon the road, Little John and the black knight riding ahead and the others following afoot.

CHAPTER FIFTEEN

A GREENWOOD GUEST

A FULL MOON hung low, yet brilliant, over the ruins of Newstead Tower and the trees of Sherwood Forest. Here and there, behind the wooden palisade that had served to keep out the Danes, its light was reflected upon the helmet or the spear-point of a Norman man-at-arms who patrolled the outer defences. Between that and the gaunt broken walls of the castle, several trenches had been dug upon the stretch of grass where Alfred of Sherwood had once kept his sheep and oxen; and despite the fact that they had been roofed with branches, the reflection of many fires could be seen above the earthen parapets. And that betokened a circumstance that we have had cause to note before: namely, that Sir Stephen de Froy knew well his business as a soldier. He was using the palisade as an outer line, which was well supported; whereas the castle itself, or what remained of it, did duty as a central keep, upon which his men might fall back in the case of the enclosure being rushed by a sudden attack. There were other sentinels on the ramparts, though by contrast, by reason of the brightness of the moon-light, the surrounding woods seemed black as Erebus itself.

Thus, for some days now, had the situation remained; and if it was something in the nature of a stalemate, that was merely because Robin knew better than to ram his head against a wall. He would not storm brick, stone and mortar, when there were cross-bowmen on the ramparts, with foresters clad only in buckskin and Lincoln green. Sooner or later, unless a relieving force came to de Froy's help, the Normans would have to fight or starve, and in the former case they would have to fight on Robin's ground.

Some way back in the forest, though near enough to give quick support to the sentries at the first sound of a horn, was the main body of the outlaws; and here, under the great oak by Holling Well, that had been their first trysting-place, Robin

Hood with a few of his chosen friends entertained a guest—and such a guest as they had never had before, though as yet not one of them had the least idea who the black knight could be.

At Robin's high table, as he called it, Maid Marian was the only representative of her sex, though others of the band beside Sir Allen had brought wives with them into the greenwood. It was a goodly feast of roasted venison and pasties baked in huge pewter platters; and although it could not compare with the banquet that a few days before had taken place at Normanton, the black knight did full justice to all that was set before him, since he had as hearty an appetite as the friar himself and he was hungry after his ride.

"I thought to meet merry company in the greenwood," said he, raising his goblet to Marian, "but I did not dream that I would meet the fair. Of a truth, sir," he added, turning to Robin, upon whose right hand he was seated, "I have a mind to join your foresters, if you will take me and think me a likely man."

"Likely enough," said Robin, "but we are all Saxon here, and thou art a Norman by thy speech."

"Norman I may be," Richard answered, "but I have good Saxon blood in me and know how to drink a Saxon toast. *Waes hael!*" he cried, again lifting his goblet.

Robin rose to his feet, also cup in hand.

"*Drinc hael!*" he shouted. "A health to Sir Black Knight, for he will give no other name! He hath shown us that he can match our good holy clerk at the board, but that be not enough to entitle him to join our company. I think, sir," he added, turning to the knight, "you would find it easier to win your spurs in the lists than in the greenwood."

"How so?" the black knight asked. "Is there some test that I must pass before I am proved worthy to rank so high as one of your merry men?"

"Of a surety, Sir Knight. I do not take every man who comes to me, for, if I did, I would be keeping all the beggars and footpads in these shires for naught. He who would enlist under my command must match me, or one of my best men, with bow, quarter-staff or stave."

" 'Tis a practice many might adopt with some advantage,"
Richard smiled, "though there would be others who would
have fewer men at their backs. Being more Norman than
Saxon, I am no past-master, I must confess, with the weapons
you suggest. There is no man here, by any chance, who would
care to meet me with lance, battle-axe or mace?"

There followed a brief silence, at the end of which Friar
Tuck burst into laughter.

"With those who hunt the King's deer, Sir Knight," said
he, "a certain modicum, as it might be called, of discretion is
essential. *Fortitudine et prudentia*, so to speak. We strive to
combine fortitude with prudence. By the size and shape of
thee, I judge that few can stand before thee in the lists."

"*In vino veritas*," the knight replied. "You see, good holy
clerk, as well as at the trencher, I can match you in a little
Latin. But, methought, it was the challenged who always had
the choice of weapons!"

"No man ever challenged any guest of mine," said Robin,
"but if in truth you wish to join us, you must first be tested
in our Saxon manner, and having passed the test, be duly
christened."

"Well," said the knight, "I have heard enough of Robin
Hood never to pit myself against him as an archer. As for the
stave, good sirs, if you will pardon me, I consider that a weapon
somewhat unsuited to my knightly dignity. The quarter-staff,
however, be another matter. I have practised it, as a pastime,
though only in my boyhood, and I may have forgotten much
that I then learned. Howbeit, if it be your pleasure so to try
me, I will unburden me of this armour and meet him whom
you consider the best man among you."

A round of applause greeted this generous challenge. Goblets
and horn cups were raised again and again to the black knight's
health, and Robin had to stand up and make a gesture commanding silence.

"Never were braver words spoken under this oak tree!"
he exclaimed. "Sir Knight, it was Little John who brought
thee hither, and for that we all have him to thank, which right
heartily we do. And you must know also that there is no man
between Trent and Don—nay, even north to the Tweed—

who can better Little John at play with the quarter-staff. But, there be others here, such as Arthur-a-Bland, and even the friar himself, who can give a good account of themselves and who are more thy weight and size than I am. Therefore, since you have one advantage and I another, being well in practice, I myself will match thee."

Assisted by Allen-a-Dale, the black knight got out of his mail, threw aside his steel knee-caps, byrnie and gambeson, and stood before them in a tight-fitting jerkin and cloth-hose.

It was only when they saw him thus clad that they realised for the first time the enormous strength of the man, for he had the bones of an ox and a chest like a churn. Whether or not he could defend himself against Robin with a quarter-staff was a matter of but small concern; it was enough for them that one had come into the greenwood to be their guest that night who was more a Titan than a man.

And what followed next, when a ring was made between the roaring fires, was a fight such as the greenwood had never seen before. One can give an idea of it by describing it as a combat between a panther and rhinoceros—though these were two animals of which the men of the greenwood had never heard in their lives. For the one was quick on his feet and agile, both to strike and parry; and the other seemed insensible to blows, though he received ten times as many as he gave. Indeed, all the merrier was the bout since the great knight so evidently knew naught, or next to naught, of the pastime; and it was equally certain that, if he did get home with one of the terrific blows he dealt so blindly, he would knock Robin senseless to the ground. Indeed, at last, so fiercely did he press the attack that Robin, parrying a blow delivered straight upon his head, was forced to his knees—and Robin was no weakling. Thinking he had now gained the advantage for which he had worked so hard at the cost of many a bruise, the knight again swung the longer end of the quarter-staff downward with all his strength and weight. But Robin was on his feet in a flash, and had stepped aside, when the oaken staff struck the root of a tree and snapped in half like a reed.

"Have done!" cried Robin. "I never had better sport in all my life! And I have seen enough of thee, Sir Knight, to know thy worth. If thou hast fought in the Holy Wars, I warrant more than one Saracen Turk went down before thy axe!"

Richard stood in the centre of the glade, his legs wide parted, breathing heavily, and with the firelight on his face. There was a light, too, in his blue eyes, and a certain fierceness in his expression that suggested he was for going on with the business. Then he looked at the broken quarter-staff he held in his hand, and with an oath hurled it into the nearest fire.

"If this be sport, as you say," he growled, "then it is of the same kind as bull-baiting. By the devil and all his imps, I am bruised from waist to head, and never to my knowledge did I get one stroke truly home."

"And well enough for me," said Robin, laughing and pointing to the ground, "else I would be lying there with a skull crushed like a hazel nut! If thou still wouldst join our company, Sir Knight, then naught remains but the christening."

Friar Tuck, rolling like an empty barrel, had already betaken himself to the well, whence he returned with a bucket charged to the brim with water.

"Have I not said, my lord of Sherwood," said the knight, "that what I say I do? If I am proved worthy of the honour, enlist me in your company, in such fashion as is your custom."

If he was about to say more, he had little chance of doing so, for at that moment he was drenched in a bucketful of water that had been emptied over his head. For a moment he clenched both fists and glared round him as if he meant to strike. Then, upon a sudden, he burst into peals of laughter.

"If I be now a merry man," said he, "I must live up to the name, though I never thought to find the test so testing."

And the next moment he found they were all toasting him again with their *waes haels* and their *drinc haels*, whilst Friar Tuck was giving him some kind of blessing in doggerel Latin.

"Since thou art wetted to the skin, Sir Knight," said Robin, "we may find a dry suit to fit thee, and Little John hath one in scarlet that is not unworthy of thy rank."

But Richard scorned the offer.

"I have been drenched often enough before now," said he, "as I have been blistered by sun and sand. Take my word for it, good sirs, there is no better cure for a wetting than a cup of strong wine and a song."

"And we have a singer here who can do your honour justice," Little John declared, leading forward Allen-a-Dale, who tuned his harp whilst they gathered round the fire.

So was the evening spent in wine, ale, merriment and song; whilst, but a few hundred yards away, Sir Stephen de Froy stamped and fumed in the old burnt-out hall at Newstead, like a tiger in a cage.

They found the knight a pallet of straw in a cave they had made under the roots of an oak tree; though, before they ushered him thither, they asked him if he, too, would give them a song.

This Richard did right readily, for he had drunk more than the head of a common man could have stood, and he cared not whether he was in the White Tower of London or under the greenwood tree. He had a voice more loud than musical, but he sung with a will to Allen's accompaniment. And that was all they wanted, and the end of his singing was greeted with another roar of applause.

As for Robin Hood, he held out his hand, and received in return a grip like that of a vice.

"I have played many parts in my own day," said he, "and I have never grudged a man for keeping for himself, so long as he can, that which he will not willingly give to others. But, surely, now, Sir Knight, since you are one of us, we may have the privilege of knowing who you are?"

Richard drew himself up to his full height, looked around him, and then shrugged his massive shoulders.

"If you so wish, so be it," said he. "My name is not unknown, for it is Richard Plantagenet, and they call me King of England."

There came a gasp as in one breath from all around. Even Robin staggered back a pace or so, as if he had been struck. And then every man among them bowed his head and sank down upon a knee.

CHAPTER SIXTEEN

THE CHALLENGE

ON THE southern side, as well as on the northern—as is customary in the conformation of all valleys—of the pleasant Vale of Newstead, there is a range of tree-clad hills. It is in this dale, where the bluebells grow beneath the elms, oaks and beeches, that King Henry the Second, Richard's father, built and founded Newstead Abbey. In the days of which we have to tell, the old Saxon Tower of Newstead stood some two miles eastward of the abbey; and upon one of the hilltops to the south, on the morning after Cœur-de-lion had disclosed his identity to Robin Hood and his merry outlaws, two men stood side by side, and looked down upon the enclosure that lay between the castle and the outer palisade: a knight in black armour and a fair-haired bearded stalwart who was clad in Lincoln green.

King Richard, whose hands were bare, since he had thrust his chain-steel gauntlets under his sword-belt, snapped a finger and thumb.

"Had I but the fifty knights I left at Charnwood," said he, "I would think no more of taking that place than a castle made of butter!"

"That may be so now, my liege," Robin answered; "but you would have found it no such easy task in my good father's day. Braisse-Neuve burnt us out like so many rats, since we would not take arms in a traitor's cause."

"And, by the rood, you were in the right!" the King exclaimed. "That be why you and your knaves are all readily forgiven for offences committed against the Church and the forest laws. What need for you to obey a rebel overlord, when he is false to his own? But, tell me, Robin, be it indeed the truth that the Wolf, with his own hands, slew thy father?"

"Aye, sire, the dead and living truth! He had sworn to do so, so they say. I saw the crime with my own eyes. He never called

upon him to surrender, even though my father would have
flung the insult back at him. He just took a cross-bow from
the hands of one of his men, and with an arrow pierced the
Thane of Sherwood to the heart. Hence it came that I turned
outlaw, and live now as a king, instead of thane, in Sherwood."

"Robin," said Richard, his voice like the low growl of the
king of the beasts after whom he had been named, "whatever
you do, whatever penalties you may incur, thou canst never
be more without the law than a Norman knight who admits
the laws of chivalry and yet slays a Saxon franklin as though
he were but a hart. So he swore to kill thy father with his own
foul paws, for never a wolf had hands that I ever heard of?"

"In the great hall at Normanton, my liege, he swore it."

"Then hear Cœur-de-lion swear an oath! By Our Lady
and Saint Dunstan and the whole category of Saxon saints—
for this be a Saxon matter—as Braisse-Neuve did to Newstead
and thy father, so, by Heaven, will I, Richard, do to him! As
he burnt out Newstead Tower, so will I raze Normanton to
the ground, until there be not one single stone that stands upon
another! Yonder," he cried, pointing downward into the valley,
"centuries to come, searching among the grass and brambles,
men may, perchance, find here and there some signs that Newstead Tower once stood upon that spot—but of Normanton not
so much as a speck of dust will they find! Thus do I swear;
and rather than break that oath, I would lose my very crown."

So fiercely had the King spoken that even Robin was over-
awed, and remained silent for a moment.

"And having heard that oath," he said, "an outlaw claims
a boon of his lord and master. I have three hundred archers
at my back; and I crave, my King, that they and I bend our
bows in thy good cause and mine, when the fate of Normanton
is sealed."

Richard laid a hand upon Robin's shoulder and burst into
a hearty laugh, when a moment before he had been fiercely
scowling.

"I were a fool to refuse so stout an ally," he replied, "even
did I not know how strong that castle stands. Thou shalt be
there, Robin, and thy rogues in green; but I want none that
are not marksmen of note, such as can keep the ramparts clear

of Braisse-Neuve's bowmen, whilst my knights and men-at-arms somehow contrive to force an entrance."

"Then I can pick two hundred, each one of whom can strike a helmet at a hundred paces, though not all could split a cane, as Much and Little John can do."

"And thyself," Richard added. "But, remember, bring also that holy friar of thine, who is a man after my own heart. Tell him that after the fighting there be always feasting, and, I warrant, that will bring him quicker than a cat into a still-room!"

"In all truth!" Robin laughed. "But, know, my liege, that Friar Tuck can bend a bow with the best of us. A brown cassock hath slain the King's deer as well as Lincoln green."

"I doubt it not, for he hath a good eye for venison; but I pardon him with all the rest of ye. Howbeit, let Normanton and Braisse-Neuve wait! I have first to settle my account with de Froy in yonder burnt-out butter-tub."

"He hath no choice, but to surrender," Robin answered. "With the news Your Majesty has brought us, and the Earl of Essex marching south from York, there is none who can come to his relief, and it is certain he must be near the end of his provisions."

"More like than not," said Richard; "but nonetheless, I may not tarry here more than a single day, for there is much that I have to do. I intend to finish this business before I leave, and that must be long before sundown."

At that Robin looked doubtful for a while.

"I am in no mind to throw away the lives of those who love me," said he, "against the very walls my forebears once defended."

"Nor will I ask it of thee," Richard replied. "I know a better way than that, and moreover I know de Froy."

"A valiant knight, I'll not deny, my liege, though I think not over-much of him as a man."

"Seven times champion in the lists," the King went on, "from Ashby to Palestine. There are few who can stand before his lance, and no man is more sure of that than he. I tell you, I know him; and because I know him, I know how to bait a trap for him that he will walk into like a mouse."

Almost at once the outlaw company was mustered at three blasts from Robin's horn. They were told to have their quivers filled with shafts, in case of any treachery on the Norman's part, since they had been summoned more to behold something in the nature of a tournament than to risk their lives in combat.

By that time all the ruined castle was astir; for they had heard the horn, and the sentries on the ramparts had reported that they had seen the outlaws gathering in the forest. De Froy got in haste into his full armour, and also Sir Geoffrey Malpert; and the palisade had been manned when Robin Hood stepped forth from the woods with Little John, who was carrying a white flag of truce.

"We demand a parley," the former cried. "I am come hither to speak with Sir Stephen de Froy himself. If he cares not for that, then we will carry on the siege."

There followed a long silence, until Sir Stephen himself appeared at the head of the steps that led up to the half-demolished tower.

"What is your will?" he asked. "I am not here to bargain with an outlaw."

"Be that as it may," came Robin's quick answer. "You can bargain or starve, or again try me in a fight in the woodlands. That, Sir Knight, is for you to choose."

"And what of thy bargaining?" he asked. "What terms have ye to offer?"

"Fairer terms than ye have any right to expect. But I am empowered, by one of rank superior to you, Sir Knight, and even my lordly self, to offer you certain fixed conditions. Withdraw your men from the palisade to within the castle, and we shall not attack."

"And for what reason may I ask?"

"A good reason that you shall learn anon. I am come to offer you terms of honourable surrender for every man who serves you; but those terms you shall not hear until your soldiers have first retired to within the walls."

De Froy paused this time for no longer than a moment. He already considered the outer palisade a danger, since his men were on half rations, and more than one of them had already fallen ill. It would be wiser therefore to defend, in case of attack, the smaller circumference of the old castle itself. Though there were places where these had crumbled in the fire, even there the debris afforded sufficient cover for his bowmen.

"Though you offer me, as it were, a pig in a poke," said he, "I accept those terms. I am not too proud to confess that we are in none too happy a plight; but, I warn you, we will fight to the last man."

"There will be no need of that," said Robin, "as thou shalt see. Carry out the first part of our contract, and the rest will follow, proving that we be honourable men, though all outlaws, saving one."

Within ten minutes de Froy had withdrawn his men-at-arms, taking what precautions he could against treachery. But not an arrow was shot from the forest, and Robin and Little John with the flag of truce still stood within the grass enclosure.

When the Normans were all within the castle, most of them having climbed over the fallen brickwork, Sir Stephen himself, with Geoffrey Malpert, took post on the top of the ruined tower; whilst the green-clad outlaws were seen to be crowding along the outer side of the palisade.

Then the gateway—where Little John had been struck down by Malpert, that day when the Thane of Sherwood had been killed—was thrown open; and there rode into the enclosure a black knight upon a great black charger, who bore no coat of arms.

From the top of the tower de Froy looked down upon this newcomer in astonishment.

"What meaneth this?" he shouted. "What Norman knight —for so I take you to be—consorts with outlaws who await the hangman's rope?"

"May they wait long, then," the black knight answered, "but that be no concern of either mine or thine. My good friend, Robin Hood, hath already given thee the choice of three evils: starve, fight, or surrender."

"The last we will never do!" Sir Stephen cried.

"That I thought, for I know thee, though you have entirely forgotten me."

"Then for what reason are you here, if not to fight?" he asked. "Lead your green-clad ruffians against these walls, and few of them will live to tell the tale."

"I be no such fool, de Froy, for I know as much, or even more, of war than thou. Therefore, since you refuse to surrender, as I have said, you have no option but to come out and fight these ruffians, as you call them, or stay where you are and starve. Yet, will I give thee another choice. You are something of a champion in the lists, if I remember rightly, and it may not have occurred to you that such a matter as this may be both easily and honourably settled by the ordeal of single combat."

"Dost challenge me?" Sir Stephen shouted from the tower.

"Aye," the other cried. "And there's my gauntlet to prove it!"

So saying, he snatched the mailed glove from his hand and hurled it to the ground.

"If thou hast not a horse strong enough to carry thee," the King went on, "we merry men of the greenwood can soon see to that; for Robin Hood hath some of the best steeds that ever crossed the Yorkshire moors."

"I have a charger of my own," de Froy answered scornfully, "in fine mettle and a match for thine. Howbeit, since you wish to meet me, have I your word that, after our joust, my men and I will be allowed to march safely with our arms to Nottingham?"

"Thy men of a certainty," the black knight snapped, "but, as for thee, whether or not you will be with them, remaineth yet to be seen."

Sir Stephen laughed.

"If I know not whom you be," he said, "it is equally certain that you know not whom you challenge, for there was never a knight yet that lifted Stephen de Froy from the saddle?"

"Then," said the other, "there may be a new experience in store for thee this very day. And now let this matter be agreed and settled. If I am vanquished, you have my word and that of Robin Hood that every man of ye can go your ways through the forest unmolested. But if I win, on the other hand, the castle surrenders. Be that clearly understood?"

"It is a fair enough offer," de Froy answered; "and all here have heard the terms. Say thy prayers, for I will meet thee here and now."

At that he turned upon his heel and disappeared from view, to reappear, a few minutes later, riding through the castle gateway, mounted on a horse, his vizor closed and carrying his lance.

CHAPTER SEVENTEEN

THE WARRIOR-KING

IT WAS, as Robin had told his followers, a tourney that they had been summoned to behold; and so long as it was any kind of a fight, their Saxon hearts could want for nothing better. The men of the greenwood thronged the palisade, like any crowd along the barriers of the lists. This was Norman chivalry, and a change from their own rough sports of bull-baiting, cudgel-play and quarter-staff. There were no heralds to proclaim the laws of the tournament and announce the prowess of the knights to be engaged, nor were there trumpeters to blast a fanfare on the entry of the marshals of the field. But, sure enough, they were to witness the breaking of a lance; and there was no one among Robin's men who would wager against the King.

Sir Geoffrey Malpert, the vain knight who bore a battle-axe he had not strength enough to wield, had taken upon himself the duties of the marshal of the tourney, and presently gave the signal that had been arranged by dropping a hand in which he held a crimson silken scarf.

Richard was off the mark like a thunderbolt, charging down the slight slope in front of him. He crouched low in the saddle, with his vizor showing only just above the plain shield upon which should have been displayed his coat of arms and the rank he held in knighthood. His great weight was thrown forward over the high pommel of his saddle, and he held his lance well lowered at the charge.

De Froy had also to descend a shorter slope before he met his adversary on the higher ground between them. However, he was seen to strike home his spurs into his charger's flanks, and by reason of his lighter weight he came forward with even greater speed. It had been calculated, by those who had hailed many a champion in the lists, that the two would meet about midway between their stations, where there was a kind of level plateau. But it was now obvious, not only that de Froy would get there first, but that that was his deliberate intention.

Indeed, he gained the higher ground, tearing forward like a flash of lightning, before the King was half-way up the reverse slope. The result of this was now manifest, and a shout of triumph came from the castle walls. They would meet with Sir Stephen coming down the slope and Richard taking the hill, so that he must thereby lose the full advantage of his superior height and weight.

For the next brief moments all on either side of the enclosure, Saxon and Norman alike, held their breath. The hoofs of the two chargers drummed upon the ground—and then there came a clash that must have rung far in Newstead Vale.

It was all over in a flash, the fraction of a second. Richard took Sir Stephen's lance in the very centre of his shield, and the force of the impact sent him backward never an inch. As for his own weapon, lifting the point of it a trifle at the very moment of the crash, he fixed it between the bars of de Froy's vizor, and hurled him like a rook shot by an arrow over the haunches of his horse.

At the top of the slope, he reined in with all his strength and weight, flung the reins aside and rapidly dismounted. Drawing his great sword, he went up to his stricken foe, opened de Froy's helmet, and placed a foot upon his chest.

Standing thus, he cried out in his great voice, with his face turned toward the castle walls.

"Ye all heard our compact," he shouted. "Here lies your champion, who will enter the lists no more, for he be dead! And so dies many another rebel. I therefore call upon all who have sought refuge in the ruins of Newstead Tower to lay down their arms and surrender."

Sir Geoffrey, who was also mounted, and who was carrying

his great battle-axe, rode forward toward the black knight. When he was within arm's reach of the conqueror, he reversed the weapon in his hand, and gave the haft to Richard.

"We surrender," he declared, though no one but the King himself could hear his voice, because of the Saxon cheers all along the palisade. "I never dreamed that I would deliver into the hands of one whom I do not even know by name a weapon that has served me so well in both the Holy Land and Normandy."

Richard, whose face was still masked behind his closed vizor, threw back his head and laughed—and his laughter was, indeed, like the roar of a hungry lion.

"Malpert," he cried, "thy axe was never of more worth to thee than a bludgeon to a mouse! I know thee well for a fool and a fop, but I never thought it was in thee to play the traitor."

Sir Geoffrey had started back at the sound of a voice that seemed familiar; and when the black knight tossed his vaunted battle-axe away, as though the thing were naught but a jester's bauble, and then lifted his vizor to disclose his bearded face, the vain knight nearly fell with astonishment from off his saddle.

"By all the fiends, even Apollyon himself, it is the King!" he gasped.

"Shame on thee that thou thought me a king no longer!" Richard exclaimed. "I must spare more than one traitor before I have cleaned up this mess that men call England, and thou mayest be among them, Malpert, for none of them, had they been free to do their worst, could have wrought me less harm than thou. And, in any case," he went on, "I am sworn to pardon every man among ye."

Sir Geoffrey had dismounted and gone down upon a knee.

"I ask no mercy, my liege lord," said he.

"Aye," Richard quickly took him up, with a savage sneer. "Because ye have no need to. Worthy of knighthood thou never wert nor will be, so take it as an honour that I now make of thee a squire. Come, lift my helmet, that these gaping loons upon the castle walls may know me as I am."   •

Malpert obeyed with hands that even trembled; and in a

moment King Richard stood bareheaded before his Norman soldiers.

"I punish not those who obey the rebel overlords that pay them," Richard went on, "yet every man of ye is my prisoner by agreement. Shame that I should take as captives those who have followed me in war! Yet I doubt not that more than one of ye have served me well; and therefore even now will I give ye a free choice: ye can come forth of this castle that a traitor baron laid in ruins, either as my prisoners or my friends."

On the ruins of old Newstead Tower, after the brief hushed silence that had followed upon the King's disclosure of his identity, a murmur like the hum of many bees had run along the wall. And then there came a loud and sudden shout, which no one could mistake for other than a cry of greeting. For none of these men would willingly have taken arms, had he known that King Richard would return again to England, since with them it had been merely a matter of vassalage for such poor pay as they received.

But there was no doubt now which way their hearts inclined. The warrior-king had come back to his home again, and all they knew was that they would serve no longer on the losing side.

"Cœur-de-lion!" The shout went up. "Long live King Richard! Long live the King!"

CHAPTER EIGHTEEN

THE KING'S COUNSELLOR

THAT NIGHT, King Richard, as he had said that he must do, had to go his ways upon his own affairs—which meant that he must ride westward upon the very road by which he had come into Sherwood Forest.

But he journeyed not alone; for with him rode Robin Hood, Little John, Will Scarlet and Sir Allen-a-Dale, the leaders of the band, all mounted and followed by two hundred foresters afoot with Little Much marching at their head. And after them came the full Norman garrison of Newstead Tower, led by Sir Geoffrey Malpert.

This in itself was a force to be reckoned with; and it was in the valley between Heanor and Ilkeston that night that they fell in with Bohun's advanced guard, marching south from York.

The news having spread like wild-fire that the King had come back into his own, the High Constable had found no difficulty in bringing to heel such rebels as there were between the Tees and Pontefract. These were few enough; and when the news came that John had fled in terror from his brother, those who had been ready to uphold his cause were quick to turn their coats. Indeed, there was only one place in all England where the King's sovereign right was yet defied, and that was where the plot had first been hatched: to wit, Braisse-Neuve's strong keep upon the hill by Derby.

It may have been sheer obstinacy upon the baron's part, but it was more likely that he knew that he could expect no mercy from the King; and however it may have been, his friends fell away from him, leaving him with none but his own men-at-arms to defend the castle.

Henry Bohun, Earl of Essex and High Constable of England, joined the King the day following the second fall of Newstead Tower, and he had with him the whole garrison of York. Richard, placing himself at the head of the army, was acclaimed with cheers, before they continued their march upon the old Danish town.

They thronged Derby town that night, which they had entered by Friar Gate; and for the one and only time the men in Lincoln green mingled in the taverns with Norman men-at-arms.

Yet, before day-break, they were mustered; and the King appeared before them, fully mailed, with an esquire bearing his escutcheon, and the royal standard and trumpeters in his train. Thus he addressed a few words to them, thanked those who had been loyal to him and generously forgave those who had not; and if he seemed milder and less harsh than was his custom, it was merely because his fury burned within him like a fire.

They then set out upon the short march up the hill to Normanton, where they found the drawbridge lifted, the portcullis lowered and the ramparts crowded with the baron's men-at-arms.

At Richard's bidding, a trumpeter rode forth, sounded a blast, and then announced that it was the King's pleasure that the Baron of Normanton and Hautbray should himself appear upon the walls—which the Wolf did promptly, like an actor who had been waiting for his cue.

"If this parley means an offer of surrender," he shouted, in a voice that was like a bark, "ye who would speak with me may hold your breath."

"I have breath enough and to spare," Richard answered him. "I hold out no vain promises of mercy to such as thee, Robert Braisse-Neuve, for I am come hither to take thy life. But what may mean more to thee, I will not leave this place until Normanton be a greater ruin than a certain Saxon tower in Sherwood."

The Wolf broke into laughter.

"There are many things," he answered, "that be easier said than done. I know of no castle in this country that is stronger built or which stands upon a better site. Richard Plantagenet, if you are resolved to take this place, I am equally determined to defend it to the last or die."

"Aye, die thou shalt!" the King replied. "The trapped wolf can do naught but snarl. For myself, I think more of those who serve you; and I am wondering whether they prefer to follow Braisse-Neuve than their King. For I am not come hither to shed the blood of men who have been obedient to me in the past and toward whom I bear no grudge. I am here for you, Robert Braisse-Neuve, and you alone."

"Then, take me, if thou canst!" the Wolf shouted from the battlements. "We are ready for you; every loop-hole is manned, and we have provisions for many a month."

At that he vanished from sight, guessing the game the King was playing; for Richard was no fool, though he may not have been so cunning as the baron. He knew that he could not take the castle without serious loss of life and waste of much valuable time. He might have left Bohun to carry on the siege in whatever way he liked, whilst he himself hastened back to London, but that was never the way with Cœur-de-lion. He had therefore spoken publicly, not so much to the lord of Normanton Castle, as to those who were with him, among whom he hoped that his words and the very sight of their King in full armour might stir up dissatisfaction. If the gate was opened to him, so much the better. If not, he would break in, though a broad moat lay around the castle walls.

For two days, whilst Richard and the Earl of Essex were planning how best the castle could be captured, the fight was confined to a desultory exchange of arrows between the attackers and the besieged, who soon learned that they were opposed by no common archers.

For no Norman could show so much as the crown of his pointed helmet above the ramparts without an arrow whistling past his ear or even glancing off the iron. And then impudent and insulting messages were fixed to shafts and shot into the inner courtyards or through the embrasures.

And it so happened that an arrow struck the stones of the chapel steps, at the same moment when the Lady Beatrice Braisse-Neuve was coming from her orisons.

It is true the shaft might have struck her dead, and the tiring-maid who was with her clasped her hands and shrank back afraid. But Beatrice did no more than lift her dark eyebrows in surprise, stooped, picked up the shaft, and read what was written on the billet.

"Robin Hood!" she murmured to herself. "Marian's brother, who saved her from shame, that day in Dale Abbey!"

With that she passed on to her own bower, where a lamp burned even in daytime, since the narrow window had been bricked up as a protection.

The Wolf's only daughter, since she still would not speak to her father, had been given no option of leaving in safety before the siege began. Nor would she ask any favour of him whom she now hated and whom she had never loved. She had seen enough of Prince John, when he had been a guest for that one night within the castle walls, to know that it would be an ill day for England when such a man came to the throne. She knew, too, that the Wolf did but hope to serve his own ends by heading the insurrection; and Richard Cœur-de-lion was a name that she had honoured—and, as we have hinted, she had thought more than once of Robin Hood.

That Robin was among those who were gathered without the castle walls came as a surprise to her—and something in the nature of a shock. For she believed what she had so often heard her father say: that Normanton was impregnable, and that the walls could only be scaled over a heap of corpses that must clog the moat and rise to the very level of the ramparts. And it grieved her much to think that so much blood must be spilled in a vain and useless cause, and also that Robin Hood might be found among the dead.

However, she might have remembered Marian's words, "Thou dost not know my Robin." Nor did even King Richard know him yet, nor the Earl of Essex, nor any other of the knights and nobles who had marched south from York.

Indeed, at a council of war that was held in the house where Richard lodged, on the third evening of the siege, they were all at cross purposes. Bohun did his best to persuade the King to leave the management of the siege to him and to repair in haste to London, where he was urgently wanted by the Primate. But Richard would have none of this; he would see the matter out himself, and if he took Braisse-Neuve alive, he would string him up like a dead bird to startle crows. At that, the Earl of Salisbury declared there was naught to do but to bridge the moat and attack by night with scaling ladders.

Thus they argued for an hour or more, one suggesting this and another that; until Richard, whose temper was never slow, struck the table with a fist.

"My lords," he cried, "I know the strength of a castle when I see it, and the Wolf has done his work here passing well. I repeat to you, I cannot and I will not wait. We must storm the place, whatever the cost may prove. But, before we decide upon so desperate a venture, I have suddenly bethought me that there is one among my knights, whose opinion we have never deigned to ask."

The Earl of Essex raised his eyebrows, and looked around the room.

"And who may that be, my lord?" he asked. "We are all here, so far as I can see."

Richard lifted his great hands in mock derision.

"Woe to that unhappy country," he declaimed, "in which the High Constable is so short of sight! I see not Robin Hood."

"Robin Hood!" Bohun protested. "But, sire, the fellow be an outlaw—though I admit, he and his men have already proved their worth!"

"Outlaw or not," the King went on, "had it not been for Robert Braisse-Neuve, he would still rank as a Saxon franklin. For that alone, and because he has proved loyal to me throughout, he is deserving of a place at our council. Send for him, my lord, and tell him I command him to come hither with what dispatch he may."

Five minutes later, Robin was in the room, unarmed, but clothed in his Lincoln green.

"Be seated, Robin," said Richard, with a motion of a hand toward a vacant chair. "In the greenwood, I was one of thy lieutenants; but, in this place, thou art one of mine, and I am proud to call thee so. My lords here and myself hold a council of war, to discuss how best the castle may be taken by assault, and we can in no way come to an agreement. Hast thou thought aught upon the matter?"

"I have done more than think, Sir King," Robin promptly answered. "While you, my liege, and my lords here assembled, have been debating the matter, I, too, with my rough and ready counsellors, have thought of a device.

"It is true, alas, my lord," he continued, "I do on occasions bring down a hart; and that is why I have now an itching inclination to bring down a castle for a change."

"Indeed!" said Bohun, lifting his eyebrows even higher. "And may I ask how you propose that so simple a matter can be accomplished?"

"With my royal master's permission, I will do so," Robin bowed.

With a chuckle, Richard gave him leave.

He told them, in the first place, what they had never thought of: namely, that there were certain springs on Normanton hill, but that the supply of water that came from these was mostly used for drinking, comparatively little of it flowing into the moat.

"The water that lies between us and the castle walls be Derwent water," he went on, "and it was brought here in water carts. The baron filled the moat in spring-time; the level is now lower than it was, since there has been but little rain throughout the summer, but it is enough to serve its purpose."

By now they were all ears, Richard himself and the two earls not the least so; though it was the King who was the first to grasp what was at the back of Robin's mind.

"You mean to drain the moat!" he shouted. " 'Tis a good enough notion; but how is a trench to be dug, when there are cross-bowmen above us on the ramparts?"

"I would not trench it, my liege," said Robin, "but tunnel it, and that can incur no danger, save to one, who is willing to take the risk. The tunnel can be dug to within a few feet of the bottom of the moat. That done, one man remains within, to break down the barrier with an axe."

To a man they let out a gasp.

"And who is this man?" asked Richard. "Who in our cause would so willingly and gallantly throw away his life?"

"One which you already know well, my liege. No less a man than Little John. He hath offered himself for the work, and hath the strength to do it. But it does not follow that he must therefore lose his life. We have thought this matter out, and have come to the conclusion that, the soil being marl, once the retaining wall gives way, John will be swept down the tunnel in a wave of mud. If he can hold his breath long enough, he should be safe, for we can stand by to catch him when he is washed forth into the fresh air."

By this time, in the minds of the noble lords there present, Robin had ceased to be an outlaw; he was indeed something more than a Saxon franklin.

The King took up the tale.

"A pretty device, by my troth!" he exclaimed. "The work must be completed on a dark night, and by reason of the steep slope of the hill, the moat should run dry, or dry enough for us, in under an hour. And then we storm the place! We rush the walls with scaling ladders!"

"In my poor thinking," Robin added, "that might be more costly than a few tubs of good oil and pitch. In breaking the forest laws, my kingly master, I have learned to go stealthily and to show myself as seldom as I must. If Little John succeeds in running off the water in the moat, I see no reason why a few of my men and I should not cross the mud unseen, pack barrels of oil and pitch against the portcullis, and set afire to the gateway before the alarm be given. We must select a night when it is both dark and foggy, and for that it is the right time of year."

King Richard jumped to his feet.

"Did I not tell you, my lords," he shouted, "that there was one absent from our council who had as good a right to be here as even I myself?"

There came a murmur of applause. And that was the only occasion in the history of his adventurous life when the famous outlaw was actually shaken by the hand by the Lord High Constable of England.

CHAPTER NINETEEN

THE WOLF AND THE LION

THE DIGGING of the tunnel took more than a week; for, though there were more than eight thousand soldiers encamped around the castle walls, no more than two could work at a time, whilst a long string of others passed the earth loaded in baskets from hand to hand to the entrance.

This was some distance down the hill, for the tunnel had to be deep, as well as narrow, and cut upon a steep slope, so that the water might gush forth with all the greater violence. The place where they had begun to dig had been carefully selected behind a clump of shrubs, and in case that were not enough to prevent the workers from being seen from the ramparts, some score of tents had there been pitched close together.

The soldiery were camped on all sides, at the bottom of the hill; whereas most of the knights and their attendants had billeted themselves upon the townsfolk. As for Robin's men, they were free to come and go as they willed.

At last, at the end of those nine days or so, the captain who had been put in charge of the digging reported to the Earl of Essex that they had come to within a few feet of the bottom of the moat and that the water was already seeping through.

They had to wait two days more, for a night when there was a thick fog and the stars were shut out by clouds; and then it was that, soon after sunset, Little John set forth upon his solitary and dangerous adventure.

He was stark-naked, save for a kind of loin-cloth, and he took with him a heavy battle-axe he had borrowed from one of the knights, with which he thought he could do the work quicker than with any more homely tool. Robin was elsewhere —as we shall learn—when Little John paused at the entrance to the tunnel and laughingly told his friends that when he saw them next, he would be more like a half-drowned rat than a merry man.

They had near upon half an hour to wait—and it seemed longer to those who waited, when, at last, they heard a dull roar in the distance; and they held their breath and had counted near upon a hundred before a great gush of mud came spurting forth upon the hillside. And even then they had to wait several seconds more in grave anxiety.

They sprang upon him, like hounds upon an otter, dragged him to safety, and washed away the mire that had clogged his nose, eyes and ears. And it was a few minutes later that Robin and those with him, who were lying flat upon their faces on the moat bank, immediately opposite the drawbridge and portcullis, noticed that the level of the water had slowly begun to fall.

Under the brow of the hill Richard's Norman men-at-arms lay waiting, each stretched flat upon his face. The knights stood to their horses with their squires at hand; and among these was the King himself with the Earls of Salisbury and Essex. Behind them the lanterns were burning in the tents, so that the blurred light in the fog might suggest to the sentries on the castle turrets that life in the camp was normal—for it was still early in the night.

Thus time passed but slowly. Lower and lower sunk the

water in the moat, as Robin could tell from a plumb-line. And then, something happened that no one had foreseen: there came a kind of sucking noise as the mud squelched along the gullies in the sodden bed.

For a moment Robin feared that his whole plan might fail; and because of the noise, he thought it safe to whisper in Arthur's ear.

"If we be outdone by mud at the eleventh hour," said he, "may I never see Sherwood again."

There followed a pause before the tanner answered.

"Fear naught, Robin," said he. "Remember, we be lying with our heads downward in the moat, and therefore the noise must seem to us louder than it really is. I warrant, those above us can hear nothing, or, if they do, not one of them would guess what's amiss."

"Hist!" Robin cautioned. "Our foes are before us, not behind! How long do you think, Arthur, will it be before we can venture to cross?"

"Give it another quarter of an hour," the tanner advised. "There be naught but mud there now, and that be still draining away. So long as it is not above waist-high we can manage; but, forget not that the other slope will be slippery. If the first man falls, that will be enough to warn the wasps that we mean to burn them out."

There followed further minutes of anxious, weary waiting; and then Robin cautiously slid down the slope, supporting upon his shoulders a barrel of pitch, the wood of which had been well soaked in oil.

Gaining the bottom of the moat in safety, he found that he was standing in mud that did not reach to his knees. Arthur followed, then the friar, each with a barrel, all of which were secured to one another by means of a strong rope.

The first part of their task safely accomplished, they crossed slowly to the other bank, finding that in one place only was the mud uncomfortably deep. But the most difficult and dangerous work lay yet before them; they had to find out whether it were possible for them to scale the other side. If one of them could accomplish this, they knew that the others could follow.

It was Robin's place to lead the way; and with a thin cord

attached to his belt, he began slowly to ascend the slippery slope. This he could do only by digging holes with his feet; but, at length, he reached the top, where he grasped the stub of a tree.

The rest of it was quicker work and more easy to accomplish though the danger was as great as ever. Waiting a while and listening, Robin could hear nothing but the tramp of the feet of a sentry on the rampart over the portcullis. Then he tugged at the cord—and all went as prearranged. The last man to descend into the moat had been Stephen Pettifer, who had, wound around his waist, a good twenty feet spare of the long hempen rope that served to link the barrels. This he now unwound with one hand, whilst in the other he held the cord; and as soon as he felt Robin's tug, he cut the cord and tied the end of it to the rope.

Thus was Robin able to haul up the rope's end by means of the cord; and as soon as the former was taut and tied to the tree-stub, Martin swarmed up like a sailor, to be soon joined by the other three. And when the five of them found themselves safe and undiscovered under the very castle walls, all they had to do was to haul with all their strength and weight—and, one after the other, the barrels came sliding up the slope.

Between the foot of the castle walls and the edge of the moat there was a space that in places was not more than four yards wide; but, at the great gateway, where the portcullis had been lowered, this widened considerably; and thither, having untied the rope, each man carried his barrel, to lay it silently against the bottom of the gate.

The portcullis, as well as the gate itself, was of six-inch oak, studded with great nails and barred and pointed with iron; but they had pitch and oil enough to set fire to anything that would burn, once the flames were started.

"And now for flint and steel!" Robin whispered, as he drew a torch from his belt, the head of which had been protected from the moisture by plaited strands of flax. "As soon as the torch burns and the fire begins to spread, follow me to yonder bastion! There is a niche there where we can hide out of the firelight; and there we should see much of the fun—if those above us do not see us first."

There came the snap of the tinderbox—a spark, a flame, a burning torch, and then red fire running quickly around the rim of a tub, until the whole thing burst upon a sudden into a raging furnace whose red tongues of flame leapt upward, licking the gateway and illuminating the grim walls on either hand.

From the top of a neighbouring turret, there came a loud cry:

"To arms! To arms! The castle is attacked!"

A moment later, a trumpet blared and echoed in one of the castle courtyards, and at the same time even Robin and his four companions, crouching under the wall, could hear loud shouts, the clank of arms and armour, and the shuffling of men's feet as they rushed to hold the ramparts.

Then, but a moment after, the next thing they heard was a great cheer behind them and another shout:

"*Forward! King Richard and Saint George for England!*"

Next came the rustling sound of a swarm of crossbow-arrows that flew high above them, aimed at the ramparts and the turrets; for the King had sent forward his bowmen first, to keep the walls from being manned. And, in the meantime, the red fire at the gateway rose and spread; and by the light of it, Braisse-Neuve's soldiery learned for the first time that the moat was empty.

Nonetheless, even though they saw defeat staring them in the face, there were a few who to the last remained faithful to the baron; and these the Wolf mustered in the central courtyard upon which the gate opened, for he had seen already that the portcullis and the main gate were doomed.

Indeed, the fire had done its work. The portcullis woodwork was in flames that had spread to the gate beyond and which, mounting higher, lapped the chains of the drawbridge, which presently was itself also on fire.

Richard had foreseen that this might happen; but, in any case, he had little doubt that he and his knights would soon force an entrance, once the moat was emptied and the arched gateway cleared. But, as a matter of fact, things went better for him than he had any right to expect. The huge iron staples to which the drawbridge-chains were attached were torn out by the weight of the bridge itself from the charred and burning woodwork, with the result that suddenly the whole thing came crashing down into the moat. And so heavy was the weight of it that the soft banks on either side crumbled and fell in, to form a kind of embankment.

Steam rose in clouds from what was now no more than a shallow ditch. Embers of charcoal, red-hot studs and bars and bolts, sizzled in the mud. Clouds of smoke rolled from the gateway into the courtyard, for a wind had sprung up, and this blowing in the direction of the attack, caused the fire to spread to the inner buildings in the castle.

It also paved the way for King Richard and his knights. More than one charger refused to face the smoke, until Cœur-de-lion himself spurred his steed down the slope into the steaming moat.

The King bore in his right hand his battle-axe, whilst his great sword was unsheathed. Jamming his spurs into his horse's flanks, he rushed the reverse slope, as a huntsman takes a jump. The charger slipped, reared, and snorted at the smoke; and it was only the rider's spurs and the great strength of his left hand that held the reins that kept the animal headed for the gateway.

Once given a lead, the other horses faced the fire, with plumed knights and gallant lords in the saddle, who with swords drawn shouted for the King, whom they followed as closely as they could.

The King, having plunged into the smoke beneath the archway, the armoured noble animal he rode, being now half frenzied with fright and with hocks singed by embers, took what remained of the fallen gate and portcullis at a single leap. And a moment after, Cœur-de-lion was in the outer courtyard.

His knights, four abreast—for there was space for no more—came after him at a gallop, the hoofs of their chargers scattering and stamping out the embers underfoot. And after them came Robin and the four who were with him—for by now they had had time to recross the moat and arm themselves with both bows and swords.

Thus they were among the few who beheld the end of Robert Braisse-Neuve, Baron of Normanton and Hautbray; and if

his life had been evil and ruthless, it may be said for him that
he faced that death like one with a better conscience. In the
court, where the smoke hung in wreaths, illumined by the
burning buildings on either hand, the Wolf wheeled his steed
and, sword in hand, rushed at the charge at a man who, none
knew better than he, was the first knight in Europe. And he
went down before the weight of that great battle-axe with his
helmet crushed like a nut, and lay in his own blood under the
smoke that even then was consuming, as a tide might wash
away a castle made of sand, the strong and noble keep he had
built for himself upon the hill by Derby. 'The Lion had
triumphed over the Wolf—and even yet the flames were
spreading.

CHAPTER TWENTY

THE CALL OF THE WOODLAND

A GREAT crowd packed the bank of the moat, all gazing and
gaping at the fire that consumed all that would burn within
the strong walls of Normanton. All the garrison were said to
have escaped in safety from the conflagration, for there had
been but few who had lost their lives; they had streamed out
by the gateway through which King Richard had forced entrance
with his knights, many of them having cast away their arms,
and now they mingled with their Norman comrades, who but a
few minutes before had been their foes.

Nor were these all who watched the flames; for every moment
the crowd was swelled with the excited citizens of Derby who
came running and laughing up the hill, for they had ever
hated Robert Braisse-Neuve even more than they had feared
him.

But a little way from where the drawbridge had once spanned
the moat, Robin Hood stood with his stalwart friend, Little
John, who had now cleansed his outer self of mud and refreshed
his inner man with a draught of ale that had been brewed at
the nearby village of Burton-on-the-Trent: Stutely and Will

Scarlock were with them, and one or two others of the green-wood company, when they saw a youth who came riding towards them, forcing his way through the crowd and crying out in a somewhat high-pitched voice that they must make way for him, as he came thither on a matter of life and death.

It was Allen who was the first to recognise the rider—and, indeed, this was likely enough, for it was none other than Marian who was seated astride the horse. A man's cloak depended from her shoulders, and under that she was wearing her suit of Lincoln green.

"Hast seen Beatrice?" she cried. "Has she passed the gate, the Lady Beatrice of Normanton? I have been told, not three minutes since, that every night it was her father's custom to lock her up in the western tower!"

Robin and his fellows glanced at one another in startled amazement. Marian, swinging down from the saddle, went on, her voice trembling and her face drawn with distress.

"She must be there still!" she cried. "It is that way the fire is spreading. I know the castle well; one can only get to that turret by passing up the steps to the minstrels' gallery above the hall."

Robin tugged at his beard.

"She would have called for help from one of the windows," he suggested. "The castle is surrounded by people, and some-one must have heard her."

"No!" cried Marian, wringing her hands. "That was not possible, for I have been told that all the windows, loopholes and embrasures in that tower are bricked up against our arrows."

Robin hesitated a moment. Then he turned quickly to Stutely, and gave him a few quick orders, telling him to get a length of the rope they had used to drag the casks of oil and pitch across the moat.

"As for the rest of it," said he—and these were the only words that Marian heard, "the cord we used, fixed to a grey-goose shaft, should be enough to do the business."

At that he was off like a streak of light, across the moat at the place where once had stood the drawbridge. The others hastened after him: Little John, Will Scarlock, Marian and Allen.

The gateway was now clear of smoke, for the embers had all been trodden out. In the courtyard beyond, he halted and waited for Marian, who came up to him and clutched him by an arm.

"Which way?" Robin asked.

"Thither," she answered, pointing past the burning chapel where the roof had already fallen in. And after that, for a little while, it was Marian who led the way.

They entered a long corridor, where both walls and floor were of stone and there was naught to burn, though the atmosphere was thick with smoke. Thence they mounted some steps, and entered the hall, where the strewn rushes on the flagstones had all been consumed by the fire and were now naught but smoking ashes.

Here it was that Marian was taken on a sudden by a fit of violent coughing, whereas the eyes of all five of them were smarting from the smoke. However, holding their forearms before their faces, they continued to hasten forward, running the gauntlet of the flames, up a flight of wooden stairs to reach the gallery in safety.

Marian, unable to speak and breathing with difficulty, pointed to an open door, through which they could see the bottom of yet another burning flight of steps.

It was Little John now who held Robin back.

"Thou canst not go there, Robin!" he cried. "It looks like certain death."

"Then if I die," said Robin, "it is yourself, John, who will command in my stead. Until then, do all four of ye obey me. Get back to Will Stutely outside the western tower. And if ye see me not again, remember that I might have perished in a worse cause."

However, Little John was not destined to reign in Robin's stead, for some short time later Robin and Beatrice had joined those who were waiting for them on the banquette, on the inner side of the moat.

By then Marian had forgotten that she was one of the merry men of the greenwood; for, in the way of a woman, she had flung her arms around her friend's neck.

"Thy brother hath saved my life," Beatrice said. And then

she turned to Robin, to thank him from her heart. But Robin was gone.

He had seen a look in Beatrice's eyes that had told him he had come to the crossroads of his life. If he stayed, he knew that, with King Richard's pardon, he would in time become a law-abiding citizen, who might attend courts, masques and revels, aping the manners of some knight of Normandy or Gascoigne. But he did not stay, because he dared not, and because, during that brief moment of hesitation, he had heard the call of the greenwood; he had seen the red deer on Sherwood hills and the fallow hart drinking at the shaded woodland brook. There was his home—his home and the kingdom wherein he ruled his merry men. And therefore, fearing that those dark, soft and grateful eyes would rob him of what he had now come to regard as his heritage, as he had never yet robbed sheriff, abbot or prior, he turned sharply on his heel, and was soon lost in the crowd. He who had baited Master Hamnett, the Sheriff of Nottingham, who had held up a wedding in Dale Abbey, faced Sir Guy of Gisborne with a sword, and brought about the downfall of a Norman castle and the death of a Norman lord, now fled in haste from a pair of Norman eyes.

As he passed down the hill, he told such of his band that he met that they were to advise the others that they would all meet that day week in the glade by Holling Well.

But, before that day came, he received a message from King Richard himself, stamped with the royal seal. It was the next thing to a command, to the effect that Robin, and such others of his green-clad company as he might choose to bring, including the stout and jovial friar, should come to the court in London, where they would receive a royal welcome. Their past crimes —since so they must be called—were all forgotten and forgiven, as meed for the good service they had rendered to their King.

Nor did that day ever come; for, after but a few months in England, Cœur-de-lion was away and under arms again, at war with the Church in Normandy. And it was there, seeking treasure-trove beneath the walls of the Castle of Châlus that he swore he would level to the ground in a like manner to Braisse-Neuve's keep by Derby—that a chance arrow struck down the fierce and knightly warrior-king.

So John came to the throne in his own right, to work the wrongs he did; and it was that which, for the rest of his adventurous life, held Robin to the greenwood. Near as strong when his hair and beard were white as he had been in his youth; as an archer second to none, to the very end, and ever the friend of the homeless and oppressed, he remained the uncrowned King of Sherwood. They might hunt him from Whitby to Derby, as he hunted the royal deer, but neither Master Ronald Hamnett nor his son who succeeded him as Sheriff of Nottingham could ever lay a hand on Robin Hood. And it was during those years that the famed and daring outlaw beheld all England become as one fair united land—the beginning of that time when the Saxon and the Norman were no longer foes, when they could think alike, fight side by side, and speak in the same rich tongue.

For thus, as we said in the beginning of our story, was our England formed and moulded; and thus, because of the deeds of which we have now told, does Robin Hood, even to this day, stand for something that is English.

THE END